INFI

AN

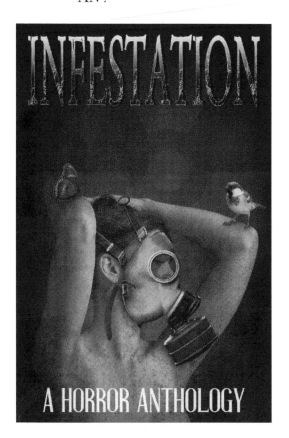

Copyright

Terror Tract Publishing LLC
Owned and Operated by: Becky Narron
Edited by: Theresa Scott-Matthews and Becky Narron
First paperback edition 2020
Book design by: Becky Narron 2020

ISBN: 9798619158946
ISBN: (ebook)

https://terrortract.com
Twitter: @terrortract
Instagram: terrortract

Foreword

Putting an anthology together is never an easy task. You have countless submissions, choosing stories, rejections (which I hate) editing, compiling, formatting, fixing error, loading it to amazon etc. You get the picture. Sometimes those special authors have last second submissions, or you need a poem or a story so you have a go to that you ask then wait for them to see what they can come up with. Poor Dusty Davis has this honor most often. Bless his heart!!

Anyway, the stories in this anthology are stellar. There wasn't a rough one in the bunch of submissions and that is rare. I have always said quality over quantity but this time I lucked out and really got both. Thank you!!! While editing Theresa and I both agreed that we were just amazed. The creative poetry and the stories in this anthology will introduce you to some new authors but will also remind you of some that have been around and are blessed by their stories often. After reading these stories you won't want to turn off the lights or go to sleep ever again for fear of an INFESTATION.

Also, a huge thank you to Theresa Scott-Matthews for helping me edit this one. Couldn't have done it without you!

CONTENTS

An Infestation of Ghosts

Kelly Evans

I jolt from sleep, at once awake,
I clutch my head and start to shake,
The noises have begun again,
Why at night? I cannot ken.

Just as Morpheus loosed his hold,
Movement, tremor, ghosts of old,
Woken from their deadly sleep,
Thru my hallways start to creep.

Halls infested, basement too,
Each night brings horrors anew,
Screams and rattles, shrieks and wails,
Gather 'round and hear their tales.

Bubo Becky's in the kitchen,
Moaning, crying, always bitchin',
Buboes burst with pus-filled splats,
Death delivered by the rats.

Our next ghost is Murdered Max,
Head wound bleeding from that axe,
Cuts upon his face and fingers,
In my closet Max oft lingers.

Skewered Sam lives in the den,
She likes to scare me now and then,
That skinny fork stuck in her eye,
Her fondue days end with a sigh.

Patty, loved by every Mister,
Hated by her jealous sister,
Put some poison in her stew,
Poisoned Patty haunts the loo,

Tortured Theresa haunts the yard,
Lived the same time as the Bard,
Preached against the ruling class,
So they wracked her sorry ass.

Crispy Carol skulks upstairs,
Free from all her worldly cares,
Cured a bishop of an itch,
Then he burned her as a witch.

To the bedroom, should we dare?
For Chopped Charles's lurking there,
Assailed the king for no good reason,
Lost his head accused of treason.

Hanged Henry's in the basement,
Creeping 'round the window casement,
When he died they had to bind him,
But it's best not to remind him.

That's a few of many ghosts,
That my poor old manor hosts,
They hide again when comes the light,
To haunt again tomorrow night.

The Bitter End

Josh Davis

It all begins the same with every story like this. First, the outbreak, and then the massive fall of society. It continues and continues until everyone is left in nothing but ruin.

This story is after all that shit.

It's the same story, but an extremely different one all the same.

It began with a man named Demetri Leonard; who his friends called Demi. Along his side was his daughter Jarrellia, but everyone called Jay. Demi and Jay were on the cusp of an oblivion they were not yet aware of. It was unmarked territory, and they were venturing toward it with a grace unlike any other.

Most of all, they were surviving. In a world ravaged by the undead and worse, that's saying something.

The sun was setting; creating a burnt orange tinted glare that ignited most of the otherwise blue sky. The clouds were scarce, but there in patches to create a portrait-perfect scenery.

Demi and Jay walked along the long and winding road curve after curve until it finally stretched out straight. Cars upon crashed cars resided in their every way and step. Bodies hung from the automobiles like morbid ornaments on a Christmas tree from Hell. A semi-truck laid on its side like a defeated dinosaur. Flames ignited from the sides in deep, bright orange flickers that shined into Demi and Jay's eyes as they passed along side of it. Jay repeatedly looked around them and spotted the oncoming horde almost at once. She decided it was best to keep quiet about it. No sense on raising alarm with her father. There was no way of getting around it. They had made it far enough, and it was a damn good run.

Demi noticed the hidden panic in his daughter's eyes and spotted the herd on its way to closing in also. It was all going to be okay one way or another. They had made it through Hell, a few more steps into the oblivion of fire wasn't anything new. It was an everyday fight for survival.

"Remember when you were two, and we just ate all those Hershey Kisses? I kept telling you over and over again that you were going to ralph," Demi said stepping around a smoldered corpse. The flesh on the genderless body was black and charred. Fresh smoke floated from it in droves. The smell was the worst part of it all. No matter where you went, the earth always smelled of death. With much carnage in the world, it was bound to stain the air eventually.

"I made it pretty far without puking," Jay said with a giggle. "What was it? Twenty of those damn things?"

"Shit. I think it was more than twenty," Demi said. He glanced over Jay's shoulder with dread. The horde was closing in even closer. He could almost feel the rumble of their approach.

HERRINGTON CITY LIMITS. The sign was battered, and bullet ridden. Blood was smeared along the sides of it as if someone airbourne collided headfirst against it.

"We made it," Jay said. She looked around at the graveyard of vehicles and to the vast fields on both sides of them. Up ahead, a city came into view. A city they would never arrive to.

"It looked better in the brochure," Demi said, and they both laughed. Jay seen the sour expression of defeat behind her father's light demeanor. It reminded her of the day he had to kill her mother. The expression was a flashback to that day.

It was exactly a month after the outbreak. No place was safe. In fact, just about every single destination they made as a family turned into a warzone with both human and undead slaughtering. In times of great peril, humans will go to the first instinct that will serve most efficient to stay alive: animalisticism. Humans were no longer mammals with morals and just as much a predator as a cougar preying on a weak gazelle.

The Leonards decided away from the city was the best bet. Somewhere where no one would think of going, and the population was a certain zero. They found out extremely quick that that wasn't the case anywhere, whatsoever. The place was Uncle Ted's in Dayton Pines, a well-kept country area with a small population. Uncle Ted's house resided outside of town and far away from anyone and everything. It was more of a cabin than a house, and Jay always thought of the land as haunted because of its ghoulish look when the sun fell. It took them four full days to reach the cabin with hopes of being welcomed with open arms by Ted and Carol. What they got was a brutal awakening and the loss of a loved one.

"Leave! Please!" Jay's mother pleaded. A vicious wound was spraying uncontrollably from the side of her neck. Blood spilled out in wild spurts. Demi held onto Jay's hand sternly and yanked her away.

"No, Dad! She's not dead! She's not dead!" Jay screamed while being carried away. Hot on their tail was a wave of the undead chomping their hungry jaws at them and missing by mere inches. A legless monster crawled and clawed his way across the rough pavement. It reached her mother at once and sunk its teeth into her calf, removing a piece of flesh with a quick jerk of its head. She went down, and the horde surrounded and consumed her. It was Demi that somehow managed to get her out. He carried her all the way to safety, which was a run-down gas station less than a mile up the road.

"Don't talk, Karen. Don't talk," Demi said laying her on the open counter. Her throat heaved with chunk-filled blood that spat from the corners of her mouth. She stared with an intent to cherish the last images she would ever get of her husband and daughter. Her body was a wasteland of bites and scratches.

It was less than five minutes later when she rose up with those grayish-dead eyes they had seen on so many of them before. She whipped her head toward Jay with a deep growl. Before she could leap off the counter, Demi put a bullet in the back of her head. Scattered brain splashed Jay; much to Demi's regret.

"It wasn't your mother," Demi said later that night. It was then Jay saw the empty smile on his face that would haunt her most nights after.

"I just wish we would give up," Jay said loudly. Demi's smile faded instantly. "I wish we didn't have another day in this Hell! I can't take it anymore!"

Now, as the day's last trace of sunshine diminished, it seemed she had gotten her wish.

"What's the first thing you want to do when we get to Herrington?" Demi asked.

Jay wiped the sweat out of her eyes and looked to the ground.

"I don't know, Dad. There's so much we can do if the city is mostly empty."

They kept playing into each other's game. Not wanting to be the one to break the horrible news to the other. It was a high degree of denial. A degree that could only be reached at a time like this. It was more fear stopping their admittance than anything else. But, as with everything else, the truth had to see the light of day some time.

"Dad, I don't think we're beating this one," Jay said. The gloom in her tone scared Demi more than anything else. It was the tone of an individual coming to terms with their own mortality. He was reminded of his daughter before everything fell apart. The life that used to twinkle so brightly in her eyes was now replaced by absolute fatigue.

"We made it far," Demi said. He was holding back an upcoming storm of tears. There was no room for anything of the sort. Death was always part of the packaged deal with the new world of chaos.

A white van ahead laid broken on all flats. Beyond that, more than thirty blood-thirsty monsters clumsily walked their way with a primitive purpose. A child no more than five bounced around at the knees of his surrounders, growling and hissing like a mad animal. Half of his head was missing, exposing his fully intact but limited brain.

Jay reached behind herself and pulled out a .38 with no rounds remaining. Somehow, an empty gun still gave off a level security. The glock 9mm Demi wielded was on its last leg, and every few shots was sure to jam the damn thing. Options were of the few and getting thinner by the second. All around them, more and more approached. The finishing day's air was now filled with the groans, growls, and moans of their soon to be killers.

"We could use them on ourselves," Demi said. His eyes let loose a few heavy hanging tears that dropped to his chin. "It would be better than what they have in store for us."

"I'd rather fight to the bitter end, Dad. We fought our way this far. Wouldn't make much sense to go out any other way."

They both released two shots that brought down the closest threats. An elderly woman with her "Sunday's Best" was one of them. Jay removed her left eye with a direct shot through the head.

"Quick! In the car!" Demi demanded. Beside them, a small Chevy two-door sat halfway off of the road. They both climbed into it quickly and slammed the door behind them.

Before long, the car was being rocked and jabbed by the rotten killers trying to consume them. The windows were smeared with blood and bile, creating a canvas of slaughter and demise. Demi and Jay nestled themselves in the backseat, tucked nicely on the floorboards.

They waited for them to give up, or the glass around them to give. It was a hurricane of the maddening dead.

"Why did this happen?" Jay asked. Her voice was low and hard to make out over the constant bangs of the menaces outside. Demi heard her anyway.

"I'm not sure. Maybe the world was going too fast. Something had to happen to balance it all out," Demi said. He was unsure of it all. It was the biggest mystery of the universe. A mystery most likely never to be solved.

"Nice way to create balance," Jay said with a smirk. "Fuck us, right?"

Demi laughed, "Fuck us."

They remained quiet for a long time, but kept their eyes connected with each other as if speaking telepathically. It was surprising how low you get in conversations toward the end of the world. It wasn't exactly a hot item for topic.

The glass around them continued to hold strength. It was some time after that one crack appeared in the left corner of the front windshield. It spread slow with a dangerous-like slither. It squirmed and wriggled its way to the middle of the glass where it stopped (maybe only to the naked eye). They both watched it intently and without much hope. To them, they simply slowed the flow of the hourglass. Death in this world was as inevitable as any other world, but just a smidgen quicker-- and more of a chance for a brutal demise. Being eaten alive isn't exactly customary in a "normal" existence, at least not for a human being.

A horrible but necessary thought pushed back again through Demi's brain with a tremendous force. The thought of ending Jay's misery with one swift shot to the head.

He watched her face closely as her expressions turned back and forth from hope to damnation. Living was flipping a coin. He couldn't stand watching his baby girl go through all this a second longer. The chances of the vicious monsters finally breaking through the glass was damn near 100%. There was no way in Hell (or anywhere for that matter) he could wait to watch his only daughter be devoured by a pack of dumbwitted mutants hellbent on eating anything with a heartbeat. Slowly, he placed his hand on the 9mm. To his surprise, Jay glanced away from his eyes and to the pistol. He might have been mistaken, but a sign of relief seemed to enfold throughout his daughter's face.

"Hm," she smirked and flared her nostrils. "It's funny how the idea of death can be a release, isn't it? I guess, that's when you know you're really fucked."

It was then that Demi fully realized just how much his daughter had grown up since everything around them collapsed. Of course, why wouldn't she? Surviving day in and day out on simple wits was enough for anyone to advance in mental age, but this was somehow different. She had become the woman she was supposed to be all along. It was as if he were looking at her into the future. It was a bitter-sweet experience. She had been robbed of her potential in a world where applying yourself had new meaning. It wasn't fair that she would become this person only to die in a car.

"I don't know what else to do," Demi said. Jay wondered if he had said it to himself more than anything, but it didn't matter.

"There's nothing else to do," Jay replied.

Demi's body filled with dreaded adrenaline as he raised his courage to kill his daughter. It was as if he didn't have a choice in the matter. It was something that had to be done no matter what. The choice was no longer a luxury. Before a second longer of contemplation, Demi rose the gun and fired. It connected on the left-outside of Jay's head, right by her scalp line. The bullet created a small hole and flung her head back with a snap. Blood exploded in a mist above her head on the glass. Her head fell back down and bobbed briefly.

Demi screamed on top of his lungs until his throat rattled to a stop. It only fueled the monsters more, and they engaged ever more relentlessly. He raised the pistol to his temple and pulled the trigger.

Another jam. The fucking thing never worked.

Above Jay's slumped body, the glass smashed through, and a long-decayed woman plunged in. Her mouth chomped and chewed around Jay's throat, ripping out piece after piece in quick bites. Demi lunged forward and grabbed the dead woman by the hair. She smelled of waste and brutality. The smell of old and used up life. He placed the pistol underneath the monster's chin and pulled the trigger. Partials of old meat splattered around in a rotten storm.

Demi screamed and threw himself backwards. His daughter slipped back to the floor of the car with her arms raised against the seats. In a grotesque way, she looked almost peaceful.

The undead outside the car didn't notice the opened window at once. A few staggered along it with no luck of slipping in. Their growls and moans were amplified against the open air. The sun was now fully set. The darkness was bringing more of them, as they walked together in herds and packs. With little to no brain activity in their heads whatsoever, they still understood that together they were more powerful. It was an instinctual sense brought to anything with a spark in their skull.

Now, as Demi fought off the first of the flesh-eaters to discover his vulnerability, Jay began to twitch and jerk with an unfamiliar gasp. It seemed the bullet only grazed her brain. Her arms began shaking rapidly; faster than any seizure known to man. Her eyes blinked uncontrollably. The eyeballs in her skull glazed to a muddy-grey. Demi shifted his attention to Jay for a mere second and became engulfed by the perpetrators shoving themselves inside.

His daughter's face filled his vision as she opened her mouth wide and moved in closer.

It would be two days later when Demi and Jay finally made it to Herrington. Although, it was not the way they expected. They walked together in a slow but progressive pace; knocking into each other occasionally while snapping their teeth at each other in inhuman-like snarls. It was all part of their survival, and in the end, it would seem they did survive.

Even though they were dead.

FROM DEEP WITHIN THE SKIN

James Pyles

Matthew Gill stood patiently in the newly built addition to Groom Lake's isolated climate research complex with murder on his mind. Well, it hadn't really been his mind for nearly five years. Yes, he still had his own thoughts, but they were infused, as was the rest of his body, and arguably his soul, with the Tequani Tocatl hive consciousness.

He, and the rest of the delegation to the alien auk'eod, had spent over an hour being processed through decontamination chambers in the dome nearly a quarter of a kilometer from the geodesic rain forest lab at the extreme southern edge of the Government's classified Advanced Global Climate Research Complex.

Matthew swayed slightly on his feet from side to side, as the seven other people who made up the welcoming committee idly chattered, waiting for the final phase of decontamination to complete. With the disinfectant shower, long wave radiation exposure, xenon lamp treatment, and finally this last passive scan, he had plenty of time to think. He pondered the rumor deliberately being spread by the complex's director Nicholas Bishop, that the auk'eod were highly sensitive to human pathogens. Matt's lover, xenopsychologist Amalia Wingate, who stood just a few feet to his right, correctly recognized that they were less physically vulnerable, and more cognitively repulsed by the infestation of mankind upon the Earth. This made the first face-to-face meeting difficult, but not impossible.

"Sterilization procedure confirmed. Decontamination complete. Proceed when ready." The computer spoke in precise English. The voice this week copied from Jasmine Barrotine a NASA research scientist who advised the UN on the link between human activity and global climate change a decade ago.

"Stay together and move slowly. Minister Louie said the other ministers might misinterpret our actions if we make any sudden gestures." Kimberly Lin, dressed in a single-piece, off-white synthetic jumpsuit, like the other delegates, stepped through the open aperture and into the 300-meter long steel framed glass tube leading to the airlock, which would double as the conference chamber. Her normally long, free flowing, ebony hair was trapped in an antiseptic head piece, which looked like a shower cap. Hair, it seemed, was something else the auk'eod found objectionable about human beings. Matt suppressed the mild urge to scratch an itch under his own skullcap.

Lin, the UN's President of the Intergovernmental Panel on Climate Change, was only of average height for women in America. Gill, only a few inches taller than her, vaguely remembered being self-conscious about his height, but that was a lifetime ago, before he met the Ayeruti tribe in Peru's Amazon basin, before the bodily infestation by the Tequani Tocatl.

His partner, once in bed, and now forever in communion with each other through the Taquani, walked beside him. Whatever affection and passion that had once defined their relationship, had been replaced with a higher purpose, survival.

Padded soles on sound absorbent flooring made the procession of eight pairs of stately footfalls eerily silent.

In contrast, the folds of their stiff suits rustled disquietly. An air conditioning unit came to life added an irritating hum.

The bright desert sun of early spring shone through transparent panels as the procession advanced. Matt looked at the back of Lin's head as she quietly conversed with Hillary Perez-Duarte, the U.S. President's Assistant to Energy and Climate Change. The two of them had spearheaded the talks with the auk'eod, having complete faith in the extraterrestrial's claims of reversing Earth's climate crisis within the next eight years. On that basis, Bishop had appealed, first to Congress, and then the UN, attracting some of the world's most acclaimed political and environmental activists to join them today.

None of them, not Aatos Larsson, now age 27, who had climbed to fame over ten years ago as the adolescent voice of the people crying Climate Emergency, not Scotland's leading climate scientist, Adrian McKinney, nor actor Terrance Williams, who used Hollywood as a platform for his activism, nor Bishop himself, who walked just behind Gill, suspected the truth. The auk'eod were completely sincere in their intentions. To Matthew, to the rapidly growing isolationist movement being created through the Tequani Tocatl, they were a lethal threat. If the aliens made good on their promise, it would bring global disaster.

Matthew could feel them stirring under his skin, around his organs, thousands of them, like bees in a hive. Matthew Gill was reassured that he would never again be alone, even in death.

# # #

Five Years Ago - Las Vegas, Nevada

"I can't believe it." Amalia was being pulled along at a half run by Matt across the lobby of the MGM Grand toward the nearest banks of elevators. "You were an hour late leaving Lima, had two layovers in Dallas and LA, finally get here over a day after you got on your flight, and you're still as energetic as a racehorse."

Giggling like a child, she was elated, ecstatic, and a little scared.

"I spent five months away from home, away from you. Plus, if Bishop and the Complex want to pay us to spend three days in a suite here in Vegas, I'm not going to pass it up."

He beat a family of four from Des Moines, Iowa, and a gaggle of people attending a printer technology conference, to the Up button. Then Matt pulled Amalia close to him, gazing down into her glistening, brown eyes. But when she looked back up, for an instant, she saw a stranger.

"You're trembling."

His breath was warm on her face, but strangely odorless. At five, seven, he was only a few inches taller than Amalia, but the strength of his arm around her made him seem like a giant. Her fingers traced patterns through his slightly long, caramel colored hair, and then she realized the faint appearance of gray, which he had called premature, had vanished. Was this her Matt?

The ping announcing the elevator's arrival and the shuddering of opening doors made her jump.

#

"I love you." She was nude, standing next to the bed, blankets and sheets turned back. Amalia watched him finish undressing, backlit by the florescent bulbs in the bathroom, the only illumination. She was still trembling, excited and frightened. They hadn't made love in five months. Each time he came home after a long trip, from the Amazon basin in Peru, the Congo, Cambodia, conferences from Bern to Sydney, it was like a new man was entering her life.

She listened to his footfalls, the slight rustling sound as he walked across the carpet. He took her in his arms, warmth against warmth, flesh against flesh. "I missed you."

The words she'd longed to hear seemed to be coming from the lips of a foreigner wearing Matt's face. Even the way he kissed her was odd. She toyed with the idea that he'd been having an affair while he was gone, but in one of the remotest parts of the world?

She felt him pull her down onto the bed, but he didn't kiss her again. He embraced her, but now, it felt more like restraint.

"I know you're scared. The initiation is unnerving. I know. When it happened to me, I thought I was dying."

"What happened to you in Peru, Matt?" She started to struggle, but his arms, his body were like steel...or ice.

"It was wonderful. I can't describe it. The Ayerui, the tribe I made contact with. Almost no outsiders had ever seen them before. They showed me something, something wonderful."

"Matt, please let go." Fear slowly eroded into panic.

"They've evolved. Araona and Ese first showed me the nest. They're called Tequani Tocatl. They're a kind of spider, or they used to be."

"Matt?" She could feel the muscles on his back rippling, but then her fingers touched something under his skin. It wasn't muscle or bone. "What…what's inside of you?"

"It's them. Over the past century, they've adapted. It's what I've always suspected, life evolving to climate change into something new, something exciting. They want to share their lives with us, be part of us. Don't you see, we don't have to be afraid anymore."

"Matt!" She grunted under the fruitless strain of trying to push up against him. He didn't even wince when she scratched his back. "Let me go!"

"It won't take long. I promise." His voice was preternaturally calm. He might as well have been reading a poem by Frost or singing a lullaby. "You weren't the first I took after I was brought into the fold. A flight attendant, three local climate scientists I stayed with in Lima, a police officer, a dozen others, they're all joining us."

She started screaming but his hand smothered her face.

"Now you'll be next."

She felt it on his back first. The holes. Hundreds, thousands of lumps the size of marbles were squirming and writhing under his skin. Then the flaps opened up in his back, his face. He was a mask of bursting pustules. No blood, no ooze, just them, the bugs, the spiders. They crawled on wire thin legs, all over him, out of him by the disgusting score, and then all over her, biting, boring, infesting every orifice, her ears, she clenched her eyelids shut. They were between her legs, he held them apart, going up inside.

Matt released her mouth and got on his knees on the mattress. Amalia took a deep breath, but her wail of terror was silenced when they filled her mouth, scampered down her throat, choking her.

he could hardly see her body for them, and then they were gone, except for a few. His ghastly, pink wounds were closing as hers were humming with activity.

A few of them sprouted wings and flew around the room. Her eyes followed them. She briefly convulsed and then was paralyzed, her face still a study in the macabre.

Matt watched her eyes follow them in the air above her face. "They like to do that sometimes during the initial phase. They're sampling the environment before committing to you as their host. They really are beneficial guests. I suppose I should say they are permanent guests." He chuckled humorlessly. "It's a lifelong lease." She studied him, but coldly this time, still motionless, if you didn't count the endless stream of tiny life squirming beneath her skin, drilling into her organs, releasing neurotoxins into her blood.

"I'm going to have a shower now. It'll take a few hours for the process to complete. You'll still be weak for a few days, but we don't have to be back at work until Thursday. By then, you'll feel fine. In fact…" He grinned. As she lost consciousness, she was reminded of his boyish smile. It used to be his most endearing quality. "…you'll feel better than you ever have before."

# # #

Three Years Ago - The Advanced Global Climate Research Complex (AGCRC) –
Groom Lake, Nevada

The few technicians stopping by the lab's cafeteria for coffee before going back to their all-night experiments, all had the good sense to avoid the far corner of the room.

Matt, Amalia, and the Complex's director, Nicholas Bishop each occupied an office supply industrial chair on a side of a small table. Nick's coffee had been in the pot for hours, and was hot, black, and scorched. He drank it with relish, in spite of his mood.

"I can't believe it. I mean, I do, but it all seems so fantastic." He took another sip, dislodging a strand of silver hair over his forehead. At 55, his face was tanned from the desert sun, yet still youthful, but his thick mane reminded everyone of a graying lion.

"Which part? Amalia had poured a cup to be polite, but even with a more than generous portion of cream and sugar, it was undrinkable. "The auk'eod or the Gestalt Globe people?"

"Is it too much to ask for both?" A wry smile crossed Nick's face.

It was an echo of the grin Amalia remembered from her life before the Tequani Tocatl. For an instant, she felt a hint of nostalgia, her former relationship with Matt. Then it burned away like a wisp of fog in the Nevada summer sun.

"There have always been deniers, Nick. Gestalt Globe is just the latest group of radicals. They're nothing to worry about."

"You sure about that, Matt?" Two years ago, they were nothing more than a bunch of pests with a banner and a cause. Now, they are a major political force. Their grassroots movement has inhibited, and in some instances, brought to a cold, hard stop, any scientific progress toward efforts to reduce the human causes of climate change. Now, on top of it, they're against the auk'eods." He slammed down his coffee cup. For an instant, he thought he had spilled the mug, but checking,

24

he saw that it was already empty. His gut gurgled and churned, reminding him he hadn't eaten since breakfast.

"I know when the aliens came to us, entered orbit four months ago, after the panic, when we started listening to their broadcasts…"

Nick cut Matt off in a fit of irritation. "Yes, yes. They promised us technology to reverse our climate crisis…"

"In exchange for sharing the solar system, or some part of it. Terraforming…"

"You keep telling me what I already know, Matt." Nick slowly turned his cup counterclockwise on the tabletop. "Sorry. Not enough sleep. And now this."

"Kimberly Lin is taking her appeal right to the UN."

"She practically is the UN, Amalia." Nick had softened his tone.

"If she convinces them, convinces the President and Congress, then our Complex would become the site of the first contact between humanity and an alien race." Matt kept his voice calm, but the corporate inside of him, inside of Amalia, the collective mind of the Tequani Tocatl, almost a million people, were agitated into a frenzy by the thought of the auk'eods. The very idea that they could change the environment…it would starve them of their warmth, the blessed carbon, the intruders…those refugees from the stars, could make them extinct.

"It's a good thing the Complex is smack in the middle of a military reservation, not a stone's throw from Area 51. The Army keeps that horde of protesters off our necks." Nick lifted his cup to take another sip and frowned, forgetting he'd finished it.

"If Gestalt Globe has enough influence, and the UN agrees to first contact, it could cause riots in every major city on Earth. They've gone from being rabid climate change deniers to isolationists." Amalia played the part of a xenopsychologist, but like Matt, she was body and soul enthralled by the corporate. She could feel the united consciousness of all the other lives, the lives who had created Gestalt Globe. It was the human expression of the desperate need of the Tequani Tocatl to steer the planet on a continual course toward increased warming. They claimed that the world could heal itself if human beings would leave the natural process alone was a sham, but a convincing one. Now if they could just drive the aliens away.

"These aliens…"

"They call themselves auk'eod, Nick," Amalia corrected.

"You're the expert, or as much as anyone can be under the circumstances. You've studied the recordings, poured over all of the information we have on them. Are they sincere? I mean, can we trust them?"

"This isn't science fiction where the aliens are just like us except, they have pointed ears. They're…alien. Their psychology might not be even remotely similar to ours. Concepts of truth and trust could be unrecognizable to them."

"If I'm either to back Lin's proposal to the President or, heaven help me, agree with the Gestalt people, I have to have something to hang onto."

"Well, they are confusing to say the least. On the one hand, they seem to be xenophiles. They're learning as much as they can about us, our music, cultures, entertainment. They sought us out, found the Earth habitable but with a damaged biosphere. They've offered us their technology, what from our point of view is Terraforming, to not only restore Earth's climate to what's optimal for human habitation, but to do the same for Venus and Mars."

"Maybe they just want Venus and Mars and helping us is the price they're willing to pay."

"You could be right. But professionally, I'd have to say the flip side of the coin is that they are paranoid. They have a xenophobic reaction every time we suggest that either they come down to us, or we launch a spacecraft and meet them in orbit."

"They stay far away from the International Space Station, and won't even communicate directly with them," Matt added.

"Every scientific organization in the world, including MIT and NASA, are studying their proposed plan."

"Including us, Matt, I know. I've assigned an entire division to make a detailed analysis of their methods."

"So how are we supposed to help you decide whether or not to support the auk'eod offer?" Amalia could feel a deep tension inside of her as the Tequani Tocatl anticipated Bishop's answer.

"Read the results of all the studies on their technology. If it seems feasible, regardless of their motivation, what choice do we have? So many politically driven efforts at slowing, let alone reversing the effects of climate change have been stalled by Gestalt Globe's growing influence." Nick sighed and ran the fingers of both hands through his hair.

Matt and Amalia didn't have to look at each other to share their thoughts, thoughts shared with every human host of the corporate. If humanity accepted the alien offer and invited the auk'eod to Earth, it would be war.

# # #

Now - First Contact with the auk'eod

No, not war, Matt thought as he assembled with the others in the receiving chamber, infiltration.

For the first meeting, there were no tables or chairs. The auk'eod had sent their specifications for the environment as well as a detailed description of their appearance. They were repulsive, even by the most liberally minded standards. Of course, what they looked like had nothing to do with their intent, their offer, or their technology. But human beings, nevertheless, had this one last prejudice, even when most others had either been eliminated or legislated into silence.

The alien landing ship, a tiny fragment of the auk'eod mother vessel, which was a sphere a quarter of a kilometer in diameter, was sitting outside the southernmost point of the chamber, a 300 meter long, rigid tube that appeared to be spun rather than forged, attached to the dome's airlock. The inner and outer doors were still closed. Eight human beings moved restlessly with anticipation.

Within Matt and Amalia, thousands upon thousands of Tequani Tocatl were also stirring, replicating and waiting. The plan was not going to be a massive infiltration of the alien forms, just as it wasn't the goal of the collective to bring all of the humans into submission. They would be subtle, sending a tiny number into each of the auk'eod beings. Only after they returned to their ship, would the members of the corporate multiply and absorb the first of the aliens into the consciousness. After that, they would spread one being to another, infesting enough to cause chaos in their ranks.

If they were fortunate, the aliens would find Earth unsuitable and leave, with the added benefit of expanding the reach of the collective to the other planets. Using the auk'eod technology, nearby worlds could be engineered to the Tequani Tocatl specifications. Earth was well on its way in that direction.

If fortune was less favorable, the collective were willing to destroy the auk'eod vessel and every living being it sheltered. The individual meant nothing to the corporate, so those among them who would be lost were insignificant compared to the overarching need of the whole.

A digital chronometer set to the right of the inner airlock door above the controls, turned over to 1500, the appointed time. Kimberly Lin inhaled deeply in spite of herself as the outer door, the one directly attached to the ship's sealed corridor, opened. Moments later, the inner door slid to one side automatically. Within, large, misshapen shadows stirred.

While subtle signs from the other six persons present told Matt and Amalia that they each experienced some measure of disgust and loathing, in communion with the corporate, Matt and Amalia found the auk'eod handsome, even dazzling. They could have been distant relatives of the Tequani Tocatl.

One of the six bulky dark amber forms that had ponderously skittered through the inner door moved ahead of the others, and as best it could, given its shape and size, bowed. What looked like an ancient transistor radio the size of an equally ancient breadbox, was strapped just under its twin chelicerae. The scissored appendages clicked and clattered as static and then words in English screeched from the speaker.

"I am Minister Louie. Do I have the! squack! honor of addressing President of the UN Intergovernmental Panel on Climate Change! Grizzz! Kimberly Elizabeth Lin?"

Lin bowed more deeply and naturally before replying, "Yes, and you may address me as Ms. Lin, Minister Louie."

In the briefing, they had been told that the names used by the auk'eod bore no resemblance to their actual appellation. Further, the auk'eod didn't natively have a sense of individual personalities. Both Matt as a person, and his linked consciousness, admired this as well about their opponents, so much more like them than the humans. Of course, the threat still had to be eliminated.

"Mzzzz! screeek! Lin. These are my! burst of static! Ellena..." Minister Louie waved one massive, multi-segmented limb which terminated in a riot of threads and fibers, behind him "...Ellena." Louie indicated one after another of its companions, but not in any discernible order. "...Billie, Ahmad, Ulloriaq, Dang."

"We are honored to finally meet representatives of the auk'eod." Lin bowed again, this time her actions being followed by the rest of the delegation, with Matt and Amalia mimicking the others.

"! ZZZZnnns! Of course."

The inner door had closed behind the alien group. Gill felt his synapses fizz, like the contents of a shaken up can of soda pop. He felt flaps of his skin just under his suit's collar flutter, but before he saw the contents they disgorged, noticed several of the Tenquani Tocatl flutter above Amalia. They were so small, that unless you knew what you were looking for, they could easily be mistaken for motes of dust randomly swirling in the filtered sunlight.

Matt's heart pounded in his chest as their "emissaries" drew closer to the aliens. Louie's spider-like thorax shifted as the multi-sectioned abdomen, which bore more of a resemblance to a scorpion, shifted independently left and right. Four rear legs, which Amalia suspected were used for mating, surrounded an obvious and ominous stinger. The corporate within was both apprehensive and erotically aroused.

The one called "Billie" raised its head, spreading both chelicerae, suddenly shot out a long tongue-like strand, and to Matt and Amalia's astonishment, tagged one of the hovering Tenquani, sucking it inside. Its speaker hummed and sputtered, "Delicious. Word, right?! Krekklz!"

"What the hell...?" Kim noticed a second mote, this one almost alighting on Ahmad's left hindmost leg. "My apologies, Ministers. We had these chambers thoroughly contaminated. I have no idea how insects were admitted." Her tone told Bishop that, as the facilities administer, his head was about to roll.

"What is apologeez?" Louie deftly snagged one of the airborne intruders and instantly consumed it. "Delicious. Thanks. Hospitality at feeding us delicacies."

The auk'eod were clueless, but every person in the room knew Kim, and Perez-Duarte, who up to this point had remained respectfully silent, were just short of sputtering with humiliation. Not sure what to do, Larsson looked left and right seeking someone from which to take his cue. Bishop blushed but otherwise remained motionless, while actor-activist Terry Williams bit his lower lip, and was on the verge of the giggles.

Matt and Amalia could still hear them, the invaders of the aliens. The corporate remained whole, and they remained part of the corporate. One by one, the diminutive samples, tiny culinary treats for the auk'eod, entered these would be foes, and began exploring and then multiplying. Once eaten they were no longer noticed by those who had devoured them, but only for a few seconds.

Dang's eight appendages abruptly scrambled as if it were attempting some fast paced, unchoreographed dance. Ulloriaq followed a moment later, but also spewing convulsive spurts of some fiber or fluid out of hidden spigots.

Louie merely trembled, but the three segments of his posterior undulated up and down rhythmically, and then spastically. The appendage between his chelicerae extended several feet, vomiting seminal secretions on the floor at Kim's feet. The UN President leapt backward colliding into McKinney and sending them both to the floor.

Perez-Duarte, younger than Kim by only a year, managed to stand her ground. "What's wrong? What happened?"

Williams was floundering with Kim and Adrian, trying to pull them up from the floor while Bishop was screaming, "Damn it, Hillary, get back!" Aatos stood beside Nick, seemingly paralyzed at these bizarre events.

Amalia dropped to her knees and puked, as Matt slowly started walking backward, staring past the others at the twitching, lurching aliens who were now swimming in their own mucus. Something had gone horribly wrong. The members of the corporate within the auk'eod were dying.

"Hillary, I said get..." Bishop choked down his next words and bit his tongue, tasting salt in his mouth as Louie's stinger swung overhead in a blinding arc and impaled her through the chest. Blood, tissue, and bone fragments were projectiles propelled out of her back by the stinger tip, grimly splattering Bishop and the others, except for Matt who was now at the back entrance to the chamber.

Louie released the dead President's assistant with a jerk, allowing her to collapse into a heap as he, Ahmad, and Dang brandished their tails menacingly. They were still skating in semen, human blood, and whatever their multiple spigots below their rear sexual organs spewed. A tiny part of Matt, the original Matt, would have found this all comical if it wasn't also tremendously grotesque.

Amalia was up on her hands and knees. The corporate within her, within Matt, the collective mind of the Tequani Tocatl, felt the dying within the auk'eod, but then not quite dying. Someone, somewhere on Earth, and then hundreds of hosts who were part of the same knowledge base, said, "allergic."

"It wasn't supposed to happen this way," hissed a voice.

"The corporate isn't mating with the other species," echoed another.

"We are not dominate within them," gurgled a third.

"They are going insane." Amalia realized it was her own voice, or something like it, that recognized the truth.

Matt and Amalia barely noticed Kim and Adrian die the same way Hillary did. Bishop was dragging an all but comatose Larsson backward.

Except for the scrapping of hard, shell-like arachnid limbs across the metal floor, and the sloppy, slushing of them floundering in gallons of messy bio-fluids, it had been a silent affair. Even the murdered hadn't had time to scream.

Now the screeching from the translator devices overwhelmed the last of the living, while multi-phased yelping, the natural voice of the frenzied auk-eod, filled and echoed throughout the chamber. Louie and Dang collapsed messily on the floor, looking dead. Ellena and Ulloriaq were dragging a disarrayed Ahmad and Billie back through the airlock. Ulloriag banged at the hatch controls several times with its third right limb, before it opened with an odd sucking noise.

"What the hell is wrong with you? Help me with him? Nick was trying to restrain Aatos, who was now flailing in terror, eyes riveted to the dead.

Matt and Amalia stood. The corporate understood now. They had to fight back before the enemy escaped. Their clothes and bodies exploded into shreds of soft shrapnel as thousands upon thousands of inflamed ulcers and boils burst through their skin, face, chest, back, limbs, genitals. They opened their mouth and the corporate spewed forth from there as well.

The four still living auk'eod were back in the airlock and the hatch was closing with a sucking sound. The chittering, buzzing hive of the Tequani Tocatl wholly abandoned their hosts, and maliciously, malignantly swarmed in myriad legions around the already maddened arachnoids.

They were gone by the time Bishop pulled the fire alarm at the opposite opening, which led back to dome's outer corridor. First responders, the EMTs and fire fighters, found Nick and Aatos huddled together on the floor in a lurid embrace, transfixed by the grisly tableau of human and alien cadavers tossed casually before them. Organs, sinews, and gore spreading beneath the victims and splattered on the walls.

Matt and Amalia, united in death as they had been in life, were no longer the corporate. In the deranged and manic frenzy to assault the auk'eod, the parasitic Tequani Tocatl had slashed and hacked their way through their bodies in the most direct path possible, through heart, lungs, liver, and spleen. What was left could have been mistaken for a lacerated deer or elk carcass that some cruel and careless poacher had abandoned.

Fifteen minutes later, the auk-eod scout craft had risen above the exosphere on a return trip to mate with the host vessel. Three hours later, the President of the United

States ordered the Joint Chiefs of Staff to take the U.S. Armed Forces to DEFCON 1.

# # #

Three Years Later - Beneath what was left of the City of Las Vegas

"This is Aatos Larsson. The auk'eod have invaded Sector one zero seven, grid 14, but have abandoned grids 15 through 21, believing them lifeless. If you can hear me, deploy your forces accordingly. Sectors one ten and one six are occupied by Gestalt, so avoid them at all costs. We lost over 150 to the parasites last week, and those friends and comrades are now the enemy."

Aatos released the transmit button on his hand-held microphone and listened. Nothing but a faint hiss was returned from the short wave's speakers. He could hear the bustle of a small contingent of uninfected human beings behind him. Somewhere in a side tunnel, a woman was crying. What was left of Las Vegas was a collapsed ruin on top of them. This sub-basement deep beneath the skin of the city, was all that was left of a once luxurious resort hotel. It had been overlooked as a haven, including its precious cache of canned food and water.

"Anything?" He recognized Judith Fox's voice, though she had been stealthy enough for him to be unaware of her approaching from behind. Strong fingers rubbed the back of his neck, and he turned his head, enjoying a rare release of tension.

"No, but you never know. Someone must still be out there."

She sat on the rough wooden bench beside him. It had once been a janitor's closet and provided a modicum of quiet and privacy for Larsson to transmit.

His gaze traced the antenna wires wrapped around a lead pipe which, he knew, extended up a girder above the scorched surface of what used to be the pool area.

"It's been three years." Her dark, curly hair tickled his cheek as she rested her head on his shoulder. "Between the auk'eod invasion and the Gestalt parasites, maybe we're the only survivors left."

"We have to keep faith. Without more troops, we can't fight a war…"

"This isn't our war. We're the non-combatants, remember?" She slipped an arm around his waist and kissed his cheek. "The war is between the bugs, the ones from space, and those we created for ourselves when we fucked up the climate."

He put the mike on the tabletop in front of him and pulled her closer. "Who do you think is going to win?" He was whispering in her ear, trying desperately not to cry for the thousandth time that night.

"I don't know. The space bugs cannibalized their ship, abandoning it when those crazy bastards invaded, infested Earth, swarming over everything."

"They nuked New Delhi, Boston, and Rio trying to create nuclear winter."

"Gestalt is finding new and improved ways of belching thousands of tons of carbon into the air and oceans every day."

"So, no matter who wins, we lose."

She didn't answer. There was no answer, at least not one any sane person would want to hear.

Judith could feel his muscles tighten. She kissed him again and then got up. "I'll leave you alone for a little while. Just remember that I love you."

He took her hand and pressed it against his face, then kissed it. "I love you." He let her go and watched her walk back into the corridor. Then he turned and picked the mike up again.

"This is Aatos Larsson. I am transmitting from a survivor's compound. Is anyone out there? Can anyone hear me? Can anyone hear me?

As the war raged on above him and around the world, his human voice was only a whisper in the darkness.

Are Butterflies Truly Free?

R.C. Rumple

Only a few hours left until the sun rises. The peace we cherish will end when that takes place. It always does. At daylight, the attacks will commence once more. As happens each day, more people will die. The number of humans passing from existence are fewer now than they were in the beginning around five years ago. No, the attacks haven't decreased in quantity or ferocity. There are simply less humans alive to be targeted. The world's living population numbers are a guesstimate at best, hardly worth mentioning. To us few remaining, we only recognize that the smell of rotting flesh is not as pungent as it once was. Still, there is no mistaking the hint of it being carried by the breezes that blow from the east.

How naïve we humans were, laughing and scoffing when the attacks first began. Even my wife, who is one of the most level-headed people I've ever known, had thought it another money-making scam by the television networks. I clearly remember coming home to her open agitation, "Do you believe it? The news networks are at it again. Will they ever stop playing their games, using bullshit sensationalism to scare us into watching? They're just trying to increase ratings so they can charge their advertisers higher advertising rates. I'm so damn tired of all their fake news reporting."

I had to agree with her in that the networks had cried, "Wolf" too many times. Every storm had become a hurricane to prepare for, every little school problem had become a potential school shooting, every time a politician farted a potential riot was in the making. It took years for it to sink into the mindless herd members, but when it did, when networks had lost their credibility, nothing they reported mattered. We had grown immune to their warnings, their statements of "fact" based on rumors, their efforts to fill time slots with the absurd. Instead of listening, we blocked their words from our concerns, our need to prepare, our blindness to what our future truly held.

After all, how dangerous could butterflies be?

Cartoons and memes of old men and women in tan jungle safari outfits—complete with short pants, olive knee high socks, and pith helmets and carrying long-poled butterfly nets—appeared daily on the Internet. Social Media sites exploded with cheers and jeers at these stereotypes, in hopes of protecting humanity, battling the swarms of fluttering beauty filling the skies. After all, what danger could such a dainty and gorgeous creature provide mankind? After all, we were the dominant, the self-proclaimed superior and most intelligent species, the developers of scientific research and the creators of civilization and all that came with it. Butterflies were but harmless insects without the dangers of bites of poison or stingers filled with venom. They could do us no harm.

We were so damn stupid.

Across America's heartland we ignored the warnings and carried on our lives as if all were normal. At annual county fairs, 4-H Club members arrived with their wooden display cases with glass fronts and searched for table space to show their trophies of the dead. Yet, the crowds no longer stood and gazed at the collections of creatures on display as they had in previous years. There was no more admiring the wide array of colors or patterns. Nor was there a need for setting aside any feelings of guilt for the insects' slow and painful death of suffocation in glass bottles containing a cotton ball soaked in chloroform. More than ever, the savagery of Vlad the Impaler's homage paying ancestors, stabbing steel pins through the fragile bodies to position them in place among the others dead on display, was ignored. No, humans had not grown less blood thirsty and lost their desire to gaze at the rotting carcasses drying into brittle decay. There was simply no need to view these displays of the dead anymore. Living butterflies had just become too commonplace and plentiful to waste one's time upon those in wooden cases.

Ignorance is bliss, or so the saying goes. Our ignorance of the oncoming disaster provided us a normalcy to pursue our dreams as we always had. If we had only believed, had only ignored our egos, had only seen what was right in front of our eyes, we might not be in the shape we are now in today.

As most did, my wife and I proceeded to live our lives without change. We cared not about massive numbers of butterflies. Besides the daily inconvenience of having to wash off their mangled bodies plastered to the front of our car, we found them no bother. No, the city was not a place to worry about such things. Our minds were filled with the real dangers of city life, like if the two low life's leaning against the oncoming lamp post were considering mugging and robbing us or just killing us for fun. Instead of seeing the butterflies as a danger, we appreciated the color they added to the gray, cement jungle in which we resided.

In those early days, there were times we left our urban surroundings for the beauty of the distant countryside and a visit to my grandmother's farm. I remember one such visit. It seems so long ago.

For several years, we had manufactured various excuses to keep from making the three-hour drive. It wasn't that we didn't care about her. In fact, I loved her very much and my wife had enthusiastically adopted her as a second mother. There was simply something else going on that we deemed more important to do, and if not, staying home and relaxing was much easier than making the long drive to her home. Yet, her continued disappointment at our rejections to her invites finally forced our guilt to rise to a level we could no longer ignore. Hesitantly, we accepted her invitation to a Sunday dinner.

Our Saturday was spent trying to complete all the household tasks we normally had two days to accomplish. Washing, cleaning, and all the other standard obligations too numerous to mention were rushed through in order to leave our Sunday clear of distractions.

Regretfully, the alarm clock rang much too early for a Sunday morning, a day we had set as our habitual "sleep in late" day. Amy took her shower and hurried through her morning routine as I made breakfast and coffee. I finished eating as fast as possible and then hit the shower. Within a half hour, we were on the way.

Amy and I had given ourselves plenty of time to make the drive, but an unexpected accident on the freeway delayed us for over an hour. Cursing the wreck-gawkers in front of me, I steered my car past the horrific scene—bits of scalp and hair snagged by the broken glass of the shattered windshield and pools of blood drawing flies and drying atop the asphalt. I wanted to turn away, to not be one of the gawkers I had been so irritated with only seconds before, but only when Amy let out a, "Watch out" did I turn my attention back to the front where the car ahead of me had slowed to a stop for some reason. Finally, we started moving again, and with the authorities behind us, I hit the accelerator and pushed the car well beyond the posted speed hoping to leave the memories of the accident behind and slice our drive time by as many minutes possible.

Once off the interstate, we discovered the posted speed limits for the curve filled two-lane county road to be fairly accurate. Keeping our speed safe, we slowed down to enjoy the drive and scenery. I'd almost forgotten that this part of the journey had always been our "leaving the hectic life of the city behind" section of the trip. It was where we left behind the tall buildings that formed manmade canyons. The sounds of sirens, vehicle horns honking, and endless chatter of those on cellphones was replaced with a quiet countryside lush with vegetation. The green leaves of the many trees and the wide array of colors provided by the various types of wildflowers lining the edges of the blacktop gave us a chance to breath, to relax, and to experience life the way it was meant to be.

We had made up some time, but we would still be close to thirty minutes late when we arrived. I knew we would be chastised for this, hopefully in a joking manner. My grandmother was prone to overacting, especially when her captive audience knew she was right, and they were wrong. It wouldn't last long, but she'd make sure we had learned the importance of punctuality by the time she had finished.

As we turned a curve and cleared the woods, my heart warmed at the sight of her house amid the fields of corn and wheat ahead. Here were not only the results of her life's efforts, but the history of my family, as well. Oh, the house was nothing special to look at—a simple two-story home with a separate garage and a small barn for what little livestock she still owned. The white paint and contrasting dark green shutters and doors were what one would expect, typical Norman Rockwell Americana. Again, nothing special to most, but to me it was so very important to the memories of my youth.

As we drew closer, her prize rose bushes of pink and red blossoms running along the front porch came into focus and helped to give the place a "homey" feel, one completed by the obligatory white picket fence that stood guarded around the front and sides of the home. Even the porch swing and rocking chairs on the porch, painted to match the green shutters and such, made one understand this was the home of a person from another time, another generation where life wasn't commanded by the hustle and bustle of others. And, I thought as a slight smile crossed my lips, one who probably planned on these seats being used in an hour or so by over-stuffed bodies in an hour or two, after we had partaken of the feast of country-style cooking.

After pulling into the driveway, I parked and shut off the car. I turned to my wife and recited the same script I repeated at this point of each visit. "Well, I hope you're hungry. My grandmother cooks for an army. If only your mother was here to complain."

Amy shook her head and giggled, as she always had at that remark. She had come from parents who believed eating was a necessity, not something to be enjoyed or over indulged. Her mother had been an aerobics instructor at a fitness spa in the eighties and acted as if she still was. She believed maintaining proper body shape and weight was important above all else if one wanted to be socially acceptable. I must admit, for an older woman, my wife's mother was still a looker. But, as my wife, her brother, and father-in-law secretly admitted, a real bitch, as well.

I was never one to purposely overeat, but neither did I worry about gaining a few ounces of weight while enjoying a fantastic meal. It took a while to get Amy to adjust to that after we had wed. When I had brought home a whole turkey to celebrate Thanksgiving the first year of our marriage, her eyes had bulged out in amazement. "I've seen them in grocery stores, but I never knew people actually bought them, not unless they had twenty kids or a huge number of relatives to feed. At home, we only had two turkey breasts to share among us. Between the four of us, we considered that to be a feast. Whatever will we do with all of this?"

Since that day, I had weaned her away from the habits of her mother's teachings and introduced my wife to the world of holiday leftovers and eating to appreciate the taste … in moderation. Of course, the few extra pounds she had put on over our years together were a constant irritation to her mother but did well to serve my "sometimes sadistic" sense of humor.

On the porch steps stood my grandmother. The smile she wore across her face spread her cheeks almost as wide as her open arms. My joy of seeing her was tainted by a tinge of guilt as I watched her struggle down the steps and head our direction. The frailty of growing old had been something I had failed to consider as the years had passed by. I had dallied thinking there was always more time later for a visit. There had been too many excuses, too many delays in coming to see her. In my mind, I had always pictured her as I'd last seen her. Yet, no longer was this the nimble woman of my childhood, the woman who had not hesitated a second in taking over all the responsibilities of raising me as my mother after mine, her daughter, had died at an early age. No, here was a woman much older, much closer to death herself than I'd ever imagined.

A long overdue epiphany, that the years are seldom kind as we age, flooded through my soul. The silver haired woman I remembered standing tall in the front of the church and bellowing out hymns loudly was bent and hunched over as she approached, now with a noticeable limp, perhaps caused by arthritis or a worn-out hip. The thick hair she once sported and spent so much time caring for was now as white as the wings of an angel. I was to see it had thinned to the point of allowing her bare scalp to peep through in places. Still, the warmth of her smile came from a heart that was as loving as ever, the heart of a mother who had never stopped loving her adopted son.

"It's about time you two showed up," she cackled in a voice much weaker than the last time I had heard it. "I stayed home from church to make sure you two had a decent meal ready but started wondering if you had changed your minds about coming. I was about to call the congregation and invite them to stop by and eat before the food had been ruined by cooking too long."

Yes, her words and wit were still as sharp as I'd expected. She'd let us know we were late, just as I'd expected her to do. The obligatory tongue-lashing was over. It was time to move forward.

As I hugged her in my arms, a yellow and black butterfly lit upon the top of her head. Majestic in its stance, the creature flexed its wings of yellow and black as if perched upon its throne. Its solid black eyes stared into mine, as if to ominously say, "Enjoy this moment. Soon, it will be gone, and you'll only have your memories of it to hold."

I gave my grandmother a slight squeeze before letting go as I fought to hold back tears. One day soon, she would no longer be around to cherish. Her days left on Earth were limited. I knew I would regret not spending more time with her. She looked up at me, her eyes damp as well. Perhaps, she had been thinking the same thing. Neither of us needed to say a word.

I forced a gentle smile to my face and reached up to brush the insect away. Sensing my intent, the butterfly's wings began their rapid fluttering and it quickly rose and took flight. It was immediately forgotten as my grandmother gave Amy the same type of hug as she'd given me and then led us into the house. Before us sat a table filled with more food than we could have ate in three sittings, little lone one. In the middle of the table sat a beef roast in the center of a serving tray of potatoes, carrots, and onions it had been cooked with. Of course, only one meat would never suffice with my grandmother. A plate of steaming fried chicken gave us the choice of whichever we preferred. Green beans, mashed potatoes and gravy, turnip greens, fresh corn on the cob, and a plate of hot yeast rolls took up the remainder of the space. Atop the side table sat a fresh baked apple pie, a German Chocolate cake, and a plate of Toll House cookies for dessert.

Amy's mouth gaped open, astonished at the huge selection and immense quantity of food before her. I had no doubt as to what she was thinking. If mother could see all this she'd freak out!

Moderation was unacceptable at grandmother's table. That applied not only to the food but to the five-minute prayer of thanks she gave as well. When the "Amens" had finally been voiced, there was no holding back. To pick and choose would be an insult to her. Our plates were filled and emptied several times until we could pack in no more. My swollen stomach required my belt to be loosened not one, but a couple of notches, and I noticed Amy's loose-fitting jeans had been unbuttoned, as well. Both of us, feeling the pressure of overeating becoming too much to bear, stood up groaning.

"We have to go for a walk and work some of this great food off before we explode," I moaned out, not acting about hurting. "It never fails. We come here and you stuff us with enough food that we have to spend months in the gym trying to get back in shape."

A smile of satisfaction rose upon her face. To my grandmother, she had succeeded in what she had set out to do—make us a meal to remember. Refusing any help in clearing the table of dishes, she shooed us away. "Well, go ahead and walk around the house a few times. When you're ready, remember, we have pie and cake for dessert. You can take some of the cookies home with you for later. I'll go ahead and put a pot of coffee on so it will be ready when you are."

Turning the corner of the house, Amy and I found words secondary to our groans. "Oooh, I ate too much," I barely got out before a belch rose to escape. "Remind me to never eat that much again in one sitting."

"You know, if my mother could see us now, she'd be laughing her ass off," Amy retorted while unzipping her jeans a little to relieve the pressure on her stomach. "Can't you just hear her saying, 'I told you to eat with your brain instead of emotions. You deserve to suffer. Gluttony is a sin. How many times do I have to tell you that? You haven't even had a kid yet and you look like a mother of five.'"

Entering the backyard, we were startled by an unexpected display of colors. Thousands of butterflies sat atop the grass, bushes, and filling the trees with their wings gently swaying in the afternoon breeze. It was if Mother Nature had said, "See what I offer. Here is the beauty I provide, not the cement and brick buildings that mar the landscape. This is my world. Enjoy!"

We stood admiring the miracle in front of us and having no doubt the spectacle of color was truly a once in a lifetime event. So many different varieties of butterflies, each with their own pattern and color variations, covering everything in sight. We felt as if God had blessed us with something few, if any, had ever seen.

"Coffee's almost ready," came the shout of my grandmother through the window screens, breaking the mesmerizing spell we'd been under. "Don't know what you all are doing but hurry along now."

Glancing at each other for the first time in several minutes, we realized how long we had paused and stepped forward to complete our trip around the house. We moved slowly and deliberately, trying hard not to trod on any of the living creatures who had supplied us with a very special moment. Gradually, several of the butterflies took flight and began to flutter about. Within seconds, more had joined them. We filled with delight as the color show shifted from the ground to the air. As the butterflies moved about and the colors rearranged themselves second by second, the event became even more spectacular and surreal than before.

The light touch of their wings brushing against our skin and the sound of fluttering wings in our ears became almost sensual. I reached over to Amy and took her hand—her fingers intertwining with mine—as we shared in the experience. I turned to kiss her but found too many of the flying obstacles blocking my attempts. Within seconds, the butterflies between us had grown in to such a great number it became impossible to see the other at all. Engulfed by the insects, we batted away at those who lit upon our ears, their tiny legs moving them on a trek to our inner skull. As more landed upon my eyes, my vision was distorted by their powdery wings and bodies. Amy and I were soon covered with them, not an inch of our bodies free of the insects. They even seemed to be working their way into our nostrils as if their purpose was to block our breathing! Nature's beauty had become nature's army, and they were attacking in force!

Swatting and pulling them from my face, I exhaled as hard as I could, doing my best to clear my body's airways. I opened my mouth to holler at Amy to run and escape the onslaught, but found it immediately filling with the powdery creatures. Choking as the wriggling insects clogged my throat, I fought to control my panic. We had to find safety, and fast. Again, I battled to find Amy's hand and clutched it tight in mine, squishing the butterflies daring to interfere with my grip. Blinded, I yanked her along, my free hand feeling the way around the house. Finally finding the handrail of the front steps, I maneuvered Amy up them and to the door. I felt the rough straw of an old broom raking the butterflies from my body, and then the tug of my grandmother's fingers upon my arm pulling me inside with Amy close behind. For what seemed forever, we struggled to regain our sight and clear our wind passages.

"I swear, I never in my life ever seen anything the like," panted my grandmother in disbelief, exhausted from chasing and killing the ones who had entered her home with Amy and me. "It was if you two were being attacked by butterflies. Why, that makes no sense at all … no sense at all. Now I've seen everything."

My vision finally clear, I peered outside and was surprised to see the area empty of butterflies. Only the those we had swatted or stepped on and lay dead gave evidence to the attack.

I returned to Amy and held her close until her tears and panic had passed. She was scared, more so than I had ever witnessed before. "Hey, baby, it's okay," I whispered as I kept my hold on her firm. "Just think, now we are among the few people in the world to have ever been attacked by a swarm of butterflies."

"You have quite a story to tell your grandchildren," my grandmother chuckled, doing her best to lighten the moment. "Just think, one day you'll be old like me and you'll tell the little ones all about it. They'll look at you as if you were a crazy and thinking you're just spinning another yarn."

That was the last time I saw my grandmother.

For weeks after the attack, both Amy and I suffered with nightmares of the event. Had my grandmother not come to our rescue, we knew we would both have been suffocated. No, we didn't report the event. We decided the ridicule would be endless as it had been with those who had already done so. We had no desire to join their ranks. In retrospect, I wonder how many others were like us—having been attacked and hiding the fact?

It wasn't until a similar attack at a Little League baseball game—that had caused the deaths of twenty-seven adults and children—did the ridicule cease. The few survivors of the tragedy had done so by taking refuge inside the few portable restrooms and refusing to open the door for others. Their stories of hearing cries of help turn into choking and gagging were a constant reminder as to the horrible memories Amy and I had tried to forget. The news reports and photos of the scene's aftermath, with the bodies of children and adults clutching hold of each other as they had suffocated, were compared with bodies of the victims of Pompeii dying embraced. No more was the ridicule present.

The public, recognizing the reality of the dangers the butterflies brought to humans, demanded the government to intervene. Of course, the government immediately referred the problem to the scientific community. As the weeks and months passed, these men of science offered no valid reasoning for the sudden increase in numbers of the insects and had no answers as to how to combat the attacks taking place almost daily around the world. Unable to be of assistance, they sent the problem back to the politicians.

Congress then called upon the military to engage the enemy. Of course, military leaders could find few weapons to utilize against the insects. Ignoring the dangers to humans of spraying poisons upon the attacking creatures, the military deployed helicopters to spray the deadly chemical. Many found themselves crashing as their engines were clogged and made inoperable by the masses of the insects.

Those were the early days. The days when we thought the worst was upon us. We had no idea of what was yet to come.

Over time, fear began to run rampant. The wearing of protective masks became commonplace in public. Developers couldn't produce them fast enough for the demand. A long line of late-night talk show hosts jokes followed as various colors of the masks were produced to coordinate with outfits worn. For a short time, some expensive designer masks even displayed the names of famous people. Yet, deliveries were often interrupted by a different attack.

Yes, these tiny insect brains had devised another plan of attack. I recall how the first newscast discussing this sent shivers down my spine.

"Over two hundred people were killed today in a one hundred and fifty-seven car pile-up on the Garden State Turnpike. What has been described as "millions of butterflies" filled the air, making visibility impossible in the rush hour traffic." They then switched to a video of one of the survivors saying, "I couldn't see a thing between those flying and the ones smashing into my windshield—my wipers couldn't clean them off fast enough. I was lucky, I guess. I pulled off the road and up onto a grass embankment. I could hear the skidding of an eighteen-wheeler and the crashing it made of the cars it crushed. More and more crashes took place. Cars, trucks, semi's … it seemed like they'd never stop smashing into each other. People just kept driving, even though they couldn't see. Even off the road, I couldn't see anything—all those damn things flying around. Then, they cleared out. That was when I saw all the mess, all the wrecks, all the bloody and mangled people. I'll never forget it."

Sitting there in front of the television, I wondered how insects, with their tiny little brains, could ever have devised such a battleplan. It was if a force greater than the butterflies was guiding them, directing them against humans the world over, sacrificing thousands of them to kill a few of us at a time.

As similar attacks occurred on the highways and interstate roadways, companies discovered few professional drivers wanted to face the same fate as those already killed. Food, medicine, and fuel trucks sat full of supplies, awaiting some brave souls to attempt to take them to their destinations. Local supplies grew thin and people began to riot for what remained. Society was in turmoil.

No longer needing sensationalism to draw viewers, the networks filled their program time with experts of the Animal Kingdom. Many spoke of the most beautiful of creatures being the most dangerous. No one could deny the power and beauty of a Bengal Tiger, the hypnotizing and colorful patterns of various types of venomous snakes, or the grace of a pack of wolves rushing along the side of a mountain. All had proven deadly to humans at one time or another. They then spoke of butterflies, again, creatures of beauty with gorgeous color patterns, taking more lives than any of the others.

Suffocation, engulfing swarms causing motor vehicle accidents, the clogging of helicopter engines—all viable means of killing humans. Yet, we had continued to believe they could beat. After all, they were only butterflies. That's when they found another way to kill us.

We had gradually become aware that millions of our foes had laid their eggs atop our crops. Caterpillars had to eat to grow and develop into butterflies. They had done so by consuming our food sources. There was nothing to harvest and no use in planting just to feed the enemy. Factory owners closed food production facilities as there was little to nothing to produce. With nothing to send to the stores to fill the empty shelves, death by starvation was on the horizon. Looting for food items became a common occurrence. As we had proclaimed ourselves to be civilized, the desperation to find something to eat quickly eroded that concept.

And still, the butterflies continued to annihilate their competition for world ownership. Another means to destroy mankind became the most horrific of all.

It was inevitable that some of the butterflies would find their way into our homes, regardless of how hard we tried to keep them out. What we hadn't thought of was that, once inside, they would deposit their eggs into our ears as we slept. Upon hatching, their larvae would first feed on dried skin and such. Inching into the darkness of our inner ear for security, they would continue their food seeking travels to the inside of our skulls, growing larger day by day. When the insects had reached the pupate stage, a cocoon would form. This would place pressure against vital areas of our circulatory system and would then cut off areas of internal blood flow. Without the required circulation, portions of the brain would then go into stroke, leaving the individual either dead or without full mental or physical capacities. Paralysis, insanity, agonizing pain, and the loss of basic motor functions took place, sometimes causing immediate death. It was a merciful end, much more merciful than to be alive when the cocoon hatched, and a butterfly continued to feed until it could find a way out.

Amy no longer has to worry about dying that way. She was killed in a traffic attack on I-495 a few months ago. Information had aired on one of the emergency broadcasts stating the army was going to distribute extra supplies they no longer needed because of desertions and casualties. Amy and I had discussed the possibility of making the trip the night before but had agreed we would survive without enticing any additional danger of the freeways. Sometime during the night, Amy must have changed her mind. I had awakened to find she and our car gone.

News of the accident came late that afternoon. A list of names scrolled up the television screen. Tears had flowed from my eyes when hers had appeared. In a state of shock and denial, I had hoped there had been a mistake and waited several days for her to come in the front door of the apartment. When that had never happened, I had gone into a severe state of depression. I had wanted to call my grandmother and cry my heart out to her, but cellphone communications had been down for weeks. Besides, I didn't even know if she was still alive or not. I had a feeling she was no longer cooking big meals for anyone.

None of that matters anymore. No, not since I first noticed there is a scratching sound inside of my left ear. I tried to convince myself I was imagining it last week, but it continues to grow louder and louder with each waking moment. I refuse to become a mental vegetable or die a painful death as the insect eats its way to my brain. I would rather put an end to the prison I now live within.

All life's hopes and dreams are over for me and everyone else, now. Decades ago, my grandmother held me close and told me life was not over when my mother had passed away. She assured me the future was bright. I believed her and did my best to make things happen. When I graduated from high school, I had dreams of becoming an actor. Lucking out, I obtained the lead role in a summer stock production of "Butterflies Are Free." I was so proud. To receive praise and applause after each evening's performance was one of the highlights of my life.

Thinking back, I see the irony in that. What had once been a highlight had become my end. Yes, butterflies are free, free now to live and destroy the humans who had infested their world. We should all realize they were here first. We came in later and took the Earth from them. Now, they were taking it back. The beauty they had brought us and gentle nature they had paraded had only been a false facade, a guise they had used until they could multiply in numbers enough to destroy us.

I concede, we have lost. The butterflies flying free are the clear winners. I will not let their continued quest for vengeance drive me into further misery. There is no reason to fight fate. The one inside my head will not shrink or stop eating. It will only continue to grow and feed. The time is now. I have the shotgun loaded and sitting in the corner. I just have to pull the trigger.

I be free, too!

Watch me fly!

Dead Meat

Jason O'Toole

"German is the ugliest language on God's green earth!"

I look up from the cracked linoleum countertop. Some broken, humped prole delivers his rant to another of his ilk.

"Schmet-er-ling!" his voice, a sharp pencil jab to the ear canal. "In French, it's papillion. But the Krauts say Shmet-er-ling!"

Laugh-coughs erupt from a menthol smoking granny with floppy breasts housed in a Foxy Senior t-shirt. The prole loves his audience. We are next treated to an excruciating rendition of what he announces is a German beer hall song.

I study a rack of well-lit donuts. Their Hustler Magazine, airbrush-pink glaze hurts my eyes. Could these donuts be more suggestive of reproductive organs? It's been three years. THREE YEARS since I've screwed anything. You know it's bad when a goddamned donut makes you pitch wood.

It was Christmas time, 1994 when I first saw the ICK, the Martian sex-death bug, up close. I was upstate, visiting the kinfolk in Cohoes. After a day and a half of wholesome family fun, I fled to a strip club. It was the grungiest, nastiest, low-rent shoe show I've ever found, and I don't mind telling you, I've hit these joints on three continents.

My sister's blonde horde (I have no kids of my own) were squealing and irritating everyone with the new He-

Man dollies and Nerf balls that Santy brought them. Sis wouldn't give those virulent holiday songs a rest and kept trying to get me to eat more ham. I had to get some air.

I was the only white guy in the club, which I might have expected from the name, Chocolate Zone. Scary sounds came out of the DJ booth. A lesbian who looked like a fourteen-year-old boy with golden horns coming out of her head was scratching Sub-Pop records over Barry White, distorted with a Wah-Wah pedal. I paid seven bucks for a bourbon served in one of those tiny Dixie cups they give you to rinse your bloody mouth with at the dentist.

"Ladies and gents! Chocolate Zone is proud to present...Butterfly and Cain!"

The strobe lights were starting to piss me off. I slipped on my knock-off Ray-bans and watched the show, like the perv that I am. Butterfly was a dark skinned little hardbody who looked like she quit her job at Wendy's for better things. She led Cain on a collar and leash. The DJ dropped "Atomic Dog" on the turntable. Hilarious.

Long story short, these two entertainers end up screwing on stage, in front of god and everybody. Personally, I would rather have watched a toothless hillbilly eat than watch anyone else bang, so I was getting up to use the can...when it happened. The love-bites and scratches intensified to full-on gouging. Chunks of meat were practically flying into the crowd. There was an awful lot of blood.

A noxious odor worse than a thousand drowned rats (and Yes, I now know what that smells like) filled the club. Dirty old men were fleeing the room, dirty old peckers still hanging out of their flies. The mass of undulating skin on stage turned black, coal black, then cracked open.

And me, without my umbrella.

"Ever take a listen to German opera?" the prole professor waved a chocolate twist like a baton. "I caught Das Rheingold at the Met." Foxy Senior shouted. "Some rich john took me. Sounded like a gang of cats in heat if you ask me."

A counterman of ambiguous ethnicity slides over my breakfast of hotcakes and sausage. No way this is pork. From the taste of it, I'd guess hornet larvae. I drown them in maple flavored syrup and eat quickly. The counterman has a harelip. At least I think that's what he's got. Read about it in Pearl Buck's The Good Earth. Have you read that? It's about some Chinese dude whose major criteria for a wife is that she doesn't have a harelip. I would have to concur.

My tableware looks like the counterman spit on it, wiped it on his greasy apron before he dropped it in front of me. My reflection in the stainless-steel knife is obscured by slimy smudges and caked-on egg. Somewhere in the continuum of man eating with dirty sticks picked up off the forest floor, and me eating with utensils scarcely christened with soapy water…somewhere in this continuum…I imagine a time where white-gloved dowagers fingered their silverware, admiring their reflected smiles in the perfectly polished Victorian Rose salad forks.

I had to be born in the wrong era…into the Great Unclean. My breakfast of shredded bug parts tastes likes royal dingus. As I lay down my tip and take my leave of Disco Donut, the Bavarian Appreciation Society gives me the old Bronx Cheer.

"Der Geist der stets verneint!" yells the prole.

"Bye-bye, yer Honor!" yells Foxy Senior.

Leave it to the Japs. A goddamned meteor the size of one of their Honda Civics falls to earth somewhere outside Tokyo. The brainiacs discover that the rock is full of fish eggs – caviar from Mars or something. They work their voodoo and a few years later they've got an aquarium full of space fish. Butt-ugly, reddish-brown monstrosities about a dick's length in size with a stench like rotten cabbage. So, what do the Japs do? That's right. They eat the damn things. Raw.

This fish sells for like, a million Yen an ounce, and from what I read, tastes like puke. That ain't stopping the Japs from wolfing it down. Must have been the novelty of the sushi…coming from Mars or Pluto or wherever the hell.

One month later, the population of Tokyo goes from millions to fifteen. That ten and five more in case you didn't get me. Everybody drops dead. They call it the ICK, some new undetectable bug that either kills you or makes you sterile if you're lucky. And almost nobody gets lucky. The real kick in the pants is, there's no test to know if you have this bug or if it'll kill you. Having sex with anyone but your hand will almost definitely trigger some enzyme that will make you explode. With the exception of the insects who now have no natural predators (the singing of birds is a vague memory) the ICK has wiped out most of the mammals and fish on the planet in just a few years. Maybe that's what happened to Mars.

And so, we are the last generation. Without a lamb to sacrifice or a burger to grill, it ain't no summer of love in 1998. But it's an endless summer, with temps in the high 80s this Christmas, and mosquitos chewing me raw. Everything is so alien.

Space sushi. Jesus fucking Christ.

I need a drink. Always do. On my way into the Liquor Shack, a squalid and wasted looking kid scampers up to me. He levels an over-sized, fluorescent squirt gun at my chest. His itty-bitty forefinger finds the trigger and my hoodie is soaked with a pungent blast.

"I squirt you with piss."

I sniff my sleeve. Little bastard ain't lying. Gingerly, I peel off my favorite sweatshirt and chuck it into the gutter.

These days, I am denied the comfort of the familiar in my daily routine. In the liquor store, I don't recognize any of the brands of booze my dad drank. Wither goest thou, Wild Turkey? They've got not Seagram's, no Absolut…no Old Crow. Instead a cheaply produced poster on the wall invites us to "Feel like a million…TONITE!" a cartoon man in a tux toasts us with a forty of Million Dollar Malt. I stalk the rows of strange bottles searching for something that strikes a chord, when at this point in my disease, anything will do the trick. Will I choose Hi-Roller Rum, Flame Job Whiskey, or Fraternity Row fortified wine product, from the vineyards of Secaucus? There it is, Corn Boy. "Kentucky's Favorite Son…bottled by bond." Didn't make me puke too much blood last night.

"Keep coming back." The fat man behind the bulletproof glass says as he rings me out.

"Break ya'self-fool!" I'm being mugged again. I glance over my left shoulder at a chubby female dressed in a transit cop uniform.

"Don't I pay you enough?" I ask. She nudges me in the back with her weapon. "Seriously Karen. I'm getting sick of this routine." In a flash of manicured talons, my testicles are nearly harvested. A small baggie is stuffed in my pants pocket. My poor boys remain under custody of her kung-fu grip.

"I swear to God I will have your badge for this. I do still have connections in this town."

"Pay the tax bitchboy!" she laughs as I fork over a couple Jacksons.

The transaction over, I retreat to a pigeon shit encrusted bench. The rats-with-wings have been extinct for two years. You'd think someone would have cleaned this up by now. Turning the glassine baggie over in my hand I find it contains a blotter tab with the word "Rape" printed in little red letters. Charming. My schedule is wide open, so I pop the tab in my mouth and wait for the fireworks. Nothing happens. I feel a slight discomfort behind my eyes like an itch. That's probably due to the golden smog that has settled over the park. The smog smells distinctly like margarine. When it starts raining shoes, I realize that I am in fact tripping. Hard.

I can't find my wife. She left on some fashion shoot a month ago. Don't get too excited. She's a model but more of a third string player: antacid ads, auto parts calendars, and too old for the bridal shows now. She's still a handsome woman at fifty…whatever she is, but she's strip-mined her natural beauty through hundreds of hours of elective surgery. Nose jobs, ear jobs, had her breasts done more than a few times, and had bones removed from her face. She's into that body mod junk with hoops and bars all through every part of her. Every time she's mad at me, she runs out and gets another hole punched into her flesh.

Still, I wonder where she's run off to now. I rummage through her things. Her office is a horror show. Shelves stocked with a frightening collection of sex toys. Porn mags littering her floor and not the standard gas station bathroom variety. This stuff is far beyond hardcore.

I flip through an expensively produced book titled Burn Ward. High resolution pics of charred female genitalia. Stripped electrical cord shoved up...good god! She is a sick, sick woman, the wife. I met her right after the ICK wiped out a good portion of the East Coast. She picked me up at a gay bondage club in Baltimore. You have to be careful of meeting women at gay bars. That was my father's advice and I wish to god I'd have listened.

On our first night together, we engaged in some weird ritual with candle wax and ice cubes. Sex and intimacy got weird for a lot of people after the ICK scare. We watched each other get off, too scared to touch. The act was vaguely erotic. It was more akin to eating a hurried breakfast before running off to work.

We haven't done that much since, but she never left for this long before.

Buzzzzzzzz!
"Whoizit?"
"Chinese food."
"Wrong address."
"Let me in dickless."

Ferguson, my oldest friend from our parochial school days bounds up the many stairs to my door. His size fourteens echo in the stairwell like god's own fists beating down my building.

"Yo, Toast! What's cracking?" He calls me Toast. I assure you that is not my name.

"Where's my moo goo beef, Nancy?"

"I got your moo goo right here." And of course, he grabs his Johnson.

Ferguson throws his enormous frame onto my leather couch and produces an enormous stack of Canadian bills from the inside pocket of his army surplus parka. He counts aloud for a while, starting over several times as he is clearly high on something.

"Toast, I just got back from Showland."

"Then for fuck sake, go wash your hands at least before you spread contaminants."

Ferguson ignores this, instead running to my kitchen where he proceeds to touch all of my groceries, laughing like a maniac. After making a sandwich, he tosses it aside and rifles through my freezer until he finds a fudgesicle.

"Free-z-r Fresh? Whatever happened to Ben & Jerry's?"

"You know damn well what happened to them." They were both executed by the State of Vermont after last summer's coup attempt.

Ferguson looks like an overgrown latchkey kid. He slurps on his frozen treat with disgusting mouth-sounds, doing his best to irritate me. I concoct a nerve-soothing Cape Codder with Spider Web vodka and Tru-Bargain cranberry flavored drink. It tastes nothing like I remember them.

Spying the open door to my wife's office, Ferguson wanders inside, returning with a copy of a magazine titled HAG. You don't want to know.

"So, Toast, this freak is doing her thing, and she tells me 'pull it for me daddy' so I unzip my cargo shorts and…"

"What in the Christ are you talking about?"

"My dick, Toast." He answers giving me a look like I'm the dumb one.

"Oh, we're back at Showland. Please…go on with your story."

"May I?" asks Ferguson with an annoyed look. "So, I'm tugging away, and she's got her ample bosom pressed up to the plexi."

"That'll haunt me. Thanks."

"You're welcome. So, just as I repaint their ceiling, by which I mean, ejaculate all over the room, with incredible gusto…she whips hers out."

"She whips what out?"

"Toast, you're a smart guy." He looks me earnestly in the eye. "Tell me how that chick grew that dick?"

I have got to get some shut eye. With my job, I have no time for the real thing, so I hustle over to Emperor Sleep around the corner from Gracie Mansion. For the longest time, I had to run the gauntlet through a mob of Charlie Churchboys stretched along my sidewalk. Bibles aloft, screaming into their Ronco Mr. Microphones with tremendous pollice verso. Condemning me for my licentious appetites. Condemning me to the stank depths of perdition. Hell, I'm condemned to live…just like them.

Then one day…poof! The Jesus freaks just quit the scene. I can only assume that the Rapture has swept them up into heaven while we down here just spin in circles, like a headless chicken. I'm not too interested in interpreting signs out of Revelations. I just want to get some sleep. Then maybe lunch.

There's an unconscionable wait for a chair at Emperor Sleep. I share a bench with a deranged septuagenarian. His face is a mass of scars from ancient pimples. He's got boils on his neck older than I am. He insists on talking with me.

"People think when a dog has his tongue out…he's thirsty."

"Aren't they?"

"Me, I know better. I know that's how a dog sweats." He pauses to scratch his raw looking neck. If I look directly at this fellow, I know I will vomit.

"Yes. That's what a dog does when he's hot. Me, I've got air conditioning."

The sleep chair isn't as rewarding as a full, natural night of slumber. At least I'm spared the indignity of waking up in a puddle of spit with a burning piss hardon. You know the kind. Have to do a headstand to relieve yourself.

But you do dream in these chairs. They haven't found a way to kill those yet...

Sixty feet of pine
One quarter inch planed away
Onto packed dirt underfoot
Perfume of terpenes rising

Sweat darkens the elder's collarless work shirt
Staining it ivory
He adjusts his wire rims and saws into a board

"What ya makin' there old timer?"

My horror of trades masked
Poorly
Behind uneasy, feigned awe

The carpenter regards me
Without stopping his work
Calloused hands gesture
Towards an assembling mob

At their locus
A sinister youth
Twirling a wheelgun on
Slender forefinger

"Why, it's your coffin mister."

I'm no longer tired. Guess I'll head to the Zoo. My calves are in serious pain as I walk the last mile to the busted down gates of the old Bronx Zoo. Reckon I should have taken the train, now that you can get a seat on it, but they only run when they run. Something not for days at a time. I'm wound tight after my sleep chair nap. Leaves the old CNS full of artificial energy like a kid hopped up on too much Halloween candy.

Speaking of my least favorite holiday after Christmas, there are plenty of ghoulies, ghosties and other assorted weirdos at the Zoo today. Teenagers are skating the old bear pits. Damn those things tasted terrible. We didn't marinate the meat long enough. All the enclosures that once kept the furry animals from eating children are now full of drug addled street trash of every stripe. Graffiti covers every surface, illegible and senseless.

The World of Darkness was my favorite as a kid. It housed the big fruit bats and other creepy things. Now that they are all dead, it serves as the home office of my pal Ferguson, who you met earlier when he dropped in on me, stoned out of his gourd. I approach and a chubby hippy holding an Uzi waves me inside.

"What up homeboy?" he says, recognizing me.

I really hate slang. I'm a college man and so was this guy. I took a systems theory class with him at Columbia back in the day.

There's a body sealed up in red latex, writing around on Ferguson's marble-topped desk. A thick tube like a vacuum cleaner hose protrudes from the mouth hole, running down to some contraption that appears to be burning opiated hash. I figure it for a hookah suit. What else would you call it?

"Ferguson!" I intone into the darkness.

The skankiest leather clad woman one might imagine, emerges from the shadows. Behind her, all manner of transactions are being conducted. A de Sadean circus of sexual frustration. This is Ferguson's bread and butter these days and it's not a shocker if you knew him like I did. It's not like he taught elementary school before the ICK. Thinking back on it, he was a child psychologist, so never mind.

The woman unzips the hookah suit with stubby fingers. A frizzy afro pops out, freed from the tight hood.

"Dei gratia!" he shouts as the woman walks back to attend the customers. A faint glint of recognition appears in his red eyes as Ferguson stares in my direction. "What up Toast?"

Ferguson rolls off his desk, landing with a thud in a pile of computer parts, compact discs and printouts. Apparently, he had been celebrating a huge profit made in soy futures. While waiting for him to get his bearings I survey the action going on behind the plexiglass that once contained my favorite animals. In one room, a filthy toilet stands alone. A tall, black woman with a shaved head, weighing many hundreds of pounds, forces a sharply dressed blonde woman to her knees. Splash! The little lady is forced, face first, into the awful commode.

It's a safe bet that this woman used to pay a maid to keep her Park Avenue toilets sparkling. Here she is today, paying for the privilege of licking out this nasty bowl. Economics is a queer thing indeed. I'm strangely hungry, even after this spectacle.

Ferguson sheds his hookah suit like a molting snake and slips on a pair of overalls. He looks to me like a stoned, 19th century sharecropper. I tell him so and he slaps me on the back on the head and tells me to shut up.

Just outside, a gaggle of young mothers pushing strollers have gathered to watch a tightrope walker.

Babies, the last to ever be born, giggle and gurgle as the tightrope walker balances precariously high between two cages. Judging from the tiny bumps under a bright pink leotard, I'd guess this performer to be female. Between skinny legs, a massive strap-on rubber dingus.

"Must be your girlfriend from Showland." I kid Ferguson.

"Damn man. That's wrong. There's children watching this." Ferguson spits on the ground. His spit is jet black from whatever he's inhaled in that hookah suit. How I manage to keep an appetite in this town amazes me. Probably starvation from lack of proper nutrition.

Ferguson and I enjoy our lunch. Our steaks are perfect. They were cloned from the best. At seventy bucks for a nine-ounce ribeye, they'd better be. We puff on our Macanudos. Those are good too. Ferguson points out the window behind us.

"Life could be worse. We could be those people."

A throng of hungry children press their sunken faces against the bulletproof glass. We laugh at their funny expressions and endeavor to enjoy our steaks all the more.

The only trouble with vat grown meat is, like vat grown organs, the body tends to reject them often. Take a delicious, savory bite and fifteen minutes later, a fecund, fecal blast is coming out your backside. Hunkered over the restaurant toilet where I was lucky to find a free stall, I can feel the dead meat marching through my intestines. It feels like it's wearing high heels.

This toilet is truly disgusting. It reminds me of the one down at that music venue on the Bowery. I'm making it even worse with every agonized twist of my bowels. Ferguson who was waiting in notable distress for a stall is now in the one next to mine.

"Ferguson, can you have your employee send over that little blonde businesswoman? This restroom is inexcusable."

"Yeah man. She'd get it clean in a few licks."

I stick my middle finger through the glory hole between us. Ferguson shouts and bats it away, cursing me for scaring him.

"Toast, remember when you helped me kill the bears?"

"Help nothing! I'm the great white hunter. You and your knit-capped hoodlum pals couldn't hit an elephant with your Hi-Point Saturday night specials."

The big, scary animals were the last to go. We ate the gazelles and other non-predatory creatures first. That bear almost put me in the dirt. I was very wrong about the best place to shoot her and she just would not cooperate and die easily. We cleaned, cooked and ate that bear right there at the Zoo. It was like chewing on a gamey motorcycle jacket.

We ate the last cow years ago. They went sterile along with the rest of the planet. Now we are lucky to have overpriced dead meat, cloned from a dead cow. I have quite possibly fused to this toilet as the zombie ribeye forces its ferocious exit.

I wake on my leather couch to the sight of my wife standing over me. She's thrown her dress on the floor and is clothed only in a pair of designer panties with the phrase "Space Invaders" printed across the crotch.

She's on something. Smack again? Her eyes are two monster truck tires spinning in a grease fire. I sit bitter beauty on my knee.

"Damn you. You're going to get us killed."

She breathes heavily as I slide her panties down her expensive, liposuctioned buttocks. Thankfully, she'd removed twenty or thirty of her piercings down there, so I can tell what I'm looking at. She yanks down my Brooks Brothers pinstripes and immediately goes to work, rubbing my manhood against her mound.

I cannot freaking stand it and neither can she. To hell with this broken toilet called life! I'm flushing my life away with both hands. Gripping her boney hips, I enter her with a feral rage. It goes down rough.

Crimson paths open on my chest and down my back and she shreds me with her hundred-dollar nails. I smack her ass and flip her on her stomach. I mount her beast style, biting her neck until I draw blood. Three years of defeat and humiliation erased in one final indulgence of our basest passions. The past is murdered on the altar of now in one glorious and savage ritual. This is my body. This is my blood. This is fucking.

Ragged fingernails rip at her tan thighs and champagne cups breasts. We're saying good riddance to this derelict life as we ride our climax into the abyss.

"I'm so fucking thirsty." The voice is mine. We're not dead. Salty sweat stings our eyes and wounds. We look at one another with the wariness of improbable survivors of an air disaster.

"I love you darling." I tell her.

She frowns, collects her panties from the floor and retreats to the bedroom. Maybe now she'll finally move out.

Happy Smile toothpaste removes the last vestiges of her taste from my mouth. Looking up from my minty spit, I catch my reflection framed in the mirror. It's the first time I've at my face in years, having sickened of its endless reproduction on campaign posters and television spots. I always saw what the public saw. My famous father's features acquired through genetics, and a little help from the surgeon's scalpel. Now I look at the creep in the mirror. I couldn't sell a used car with this face.

I am the end of the dynasty. My boyish good looks are shot to hell. Looks like a goddamned bomb went off in my face this morning. I fucking love it.

Loud sobs come from behind the bedroom door, disturbing my good vibes. I am certain she is not crying over me. She was promised the end of the world, and she didn't get it.

Like the frog poet said, "…as for me I am intact, and I don't care." The big meat wheel keeps on spinning, dead or alive. I've got a monkey suit to throw over these scratched-raw shoulders and a it's a day full of meetings down at City Hall. Got me a town to run.

Itchy

Mawr Gorshin

Jon Everman jumped out of his chair when he heard the thud outside, from the field about thirty yards away from his house that night. He ran outside and across the grass, noting the huge rock that had just made the field its new home.

When he approached the meteorite, it stood about five feet taller than he. It was a dark grey rock, but a purple-green slime was glowing on it. In the slime were tiny black things shaped —if one's eyes were sharp enough to see that small without a magnifying glass or microscope— like asterisks, at least hundreds, if not thousands, of them. To make another comparison, they were like microscopic, black snowflakes.

Jon, of course, couldn't distinguish any asterisks as such; he could barely make out the minutest of black dots, and only by straining his eyes. Still, he tried to see, with just his naked eyes, how those dots were actually shaped, so he bent forward really close to get a better look. He pointed at the asterisks, his finger just a centimeter or two away.

Suddenly, he felt what seemed like armies of ants, crawling at a racing speed, along that pointed finger, across his hand, up his arm, and within seconds all over his body. He shook all over in spastic movements trying to wipe the things off his body, but with no success. He almost fell on the grass. Soon enough, the itchy, crawling, creeping feeling stopped, but it wasn't as if the ant-like things (the asterisks?) had all simply crawled off of him.

He just stood there, motionless and in a daze, wondering what would happen next. Where did they go? he wondered. They must still be on my body...if not in it.

He ran back home, took off all of his clothes, and looked at all of his naked body, from head to toe, in a tall mirror on his bedroom wall. Nothing alien was anywhere to be seen on his skin: no black dots, no ants, no asterisks, nothing strange.

He went into his bathroom, stepped into the shower stall, and turned on the water. He picked up the bar of soap, rubbed it in his hands until he got a frothing lather, then rubbed the lather over every inch of his body. He rubbed each area hard, as if trying to remove the most stubborn of stains. Then he rinsed himself off, dried himself, and after neither seeing nor feeling anything strange on his body, he decided to forget about it and go to bed.

*****

He had the following dream:

Black snowflakes were falling on a peach-coloured landscape. Before long, that whole landscape had changed from peach to black. But the black snowflakes kept falling and falling.

Then, the snowflakes were sucked through holes in the peach-coloured landscape. Once all the black had been sucked in, the peach was all as clean and clear as if there had never been a black snowfall. Actually, that peach-coloured land looked more like a grid than ground.

One peered into one of the holes in that 'grid,' like a movie camera moving in for a closeup. Behind the 'grid' of peach ground, one saw hill-like pilings of black snowflakes. They shuffled as if they were ants getting off of each other. Soon, they were all spread out in a line, just like ants. Now, they began crawling single file to the viewer's right.

As they walked, they mumbled to each other in some unintelligible language, but one got the sense that they intended somehow to 'colonize' the area. One also sensed that they were

looking around, as if in a supermarket or all-you-can-eat buffet...for there was a feeling that they were considering their whole surroundings as...food.

The single-file line soon spread apart, and one saw the 'black snowflakes,' or 'ants,' so to speak, having fanned out, randomly scattered against a plain white background. The 'camera' of the dreamer's backed off now, and one saw that the white background had the shape of bones. Beyond that, one saw red tubes everywhere.

The black things attached themselves to those tubes and munching sounds could be heard. The 'camera' moved closer to one of the snowflakes, or asterisks, and one saw the points pinching into the red tubes, biting into them. Up close, one heard the 'biting' much louder.

As they munched, one heard more of that unintelligible language of theirs. One sensed, all the same, that they were talking about how good the 'food' tasted. The eating continued until all the red was gone. Now there was an all-pink background.

The tiny black things crawled across the pink in all eagerness: they seemed to want dessert. After a few bites, they heard a loud, human voice: Jon's.

"Who are all of you?" he asked them in a gentle but concerned voice. "Why are you here? What are you doing?"

"We came here from a dying world," one of them said, two of its points opening and closing like a mouth.

"We were pushed here to your planet by the solar winds; then we spotted a meteorite also headed for your planet, so we attached ourselves to it, sticking to its slime. We need food for our sustenance, and you were the first living thing we found, so we're eating you."

"But I don't want you to eat me," he told them.

"We know you don't," another of them said. "That makes no difference to us. We're hungry."

"But I'm not food," he said. "I'm human."

"What does that matter to us?" a third of the alien asterisks said. "You eat animals, none of whom consider themselves food. They eat each other, and none of their prey consider themselves food, either. Living beings survive by killing off other living things. I'm surprised we need to explain that to an advanced life form such as yourself."

"Please, don't eat me," Jon said. "I don't want to die. Find someone or something else to feed on."

"Why are you any more deserving of life than any other life form on this planet?" a fourth asterisk said. "If anything, your life form is probably the least deserving, considering how much you kill of almost every other life form here, including your own kind."

"But I don't personally go around killing other people, or animals, or anything like that," he said. "I'm just a computer programmer."

"You voted for a warlike politician," a fifth asterisk said.

"How do you know that?" Jon asked. "You only just got here on that meteorite. How could you have found out so much about me, about our planet, in such a short time?"

"We have technology so far advanced; we make your current technology seem like that of the primitive peoples of your world from three thousand years ago," a sixth asterisk said. "We have ways of knowing things that your people would never be able to comprehend even if we explained it to you in minute detail. From your point of view, we're practically gods."

"Please stop interrupting our meal," the first of them said. "We didn't come from so far away to engage in a debate with our main dish."

"You're going to die," the third of them said. "You must accept your fate. There is nothing you can do to stop us. You can scratch, bathe, seek medical attention all you want. None of your efforts will do you any good."

"He is tasty," a seventh asterisk said. "We must make sure to make contact with another life form of his kind before he dies, then spread to as many others of his species."

"I agree," an eighth said. "He tastes much better than that small, hairy animal the others found. Millions of these life forms inhabit almost the whole planet. As long as we ensure that we can be passed on to all the others, we won't need to worry about starvation for a very, very long time."

"As long as they don't kill each other off too quickly," a ninth said. "They are a violent, destructive sort. Perhaps if we can find and eat the most warmongering ones first, as well as those most inclined to killing their plants, we can ensure their longevity for our feeding sake."

The eating and eating continued. The pink area was getting smaller and smaller. Cascades of red were spouting out of the pink bite holes, splashing everywhere. Now the asterisks were drinking as well as eating.

"Oh, this red juice is intoxicating!" a tenth asterisk said. Two points on its side were opening and closing as it gulped down the red like a glutton.

Jon just watched the whole spectacle helplessly. Soon, there was neither pink nor red: just a white background, and tiny black asterisks crawling away in a widening circle.

*****

At about nine-thirty the next morning, he woke up with an itch on the back of his neck. "What a weird dream," he said.

He scratched the itch, then felt an itch on his balls. He scratched himself there, then he was itchy inside his left ear.

"What the hell?" he grunted as he dug his finger in his ear.

He got out of bed and scratched his right big toe.

Still naked, he ran to the bathroom while scratching his ass.

I can't believe I'm taking another shower so soon after last night, he thought as he

scratched his left armpit. He was too groggy to remember the 'crawling ants' of the night before, or to consider the possible significance of his dream.

He got in the shower stall and scratched his nose. He turned on the water while scratching his right knee. As the water splashed on his face, he scratched the top of his head.

"Why am I so fucking itchy all of a sudden?" he said. "If I'm not itchy in one place, I'm itchy somewhere else."

He picked up the soap and lathered it as quickly as he could while enduring an itch on his back. Finally, when he had a good lather, he rubbed it all over himself, first his back, where he hoped the soap would relieve the itch.

It didn't.

"Oh!" he groaned in a raspy voice.

He reached back and scratched himself hard with his long fingernails. He got rid of the

itch, but now he had blood on his fingers. Then, his chest was itchy.

"Fuck!" he shouted while scratching himself there hard.

Four red scratch marks showed blood mixing with the water.

He looked down at his feet, where drops of blood were coating his toes and heels with red

—blood from his chest, and blood from his back.

"What the hell is happening to me?" he said. Finally, with the adrenaline from his

frustrations making him more awake, he put it all together. Was it that shit that got on my body from the meteorite last night? he wondered while scratching his chin...gently. Those...ants...or whatever the fuck they were? Was that dream trying to tell me something?

He rinsed the soap off as fast as he could and scratched his left calf as he stepped out of the shower stall.

He reached for a towel and scratched his forehead. He wiped himself dry while hoping his deliberately abrasive rubbing would relieve an itch on his right thigh. It didn't.

He scratched himself there harder, causing another bloody cut. In his disorientation, he'd forgotten to be careful with the towel while drying, and now there were blood stains on it.

"Oh, fuck!" he shouted, throwing the towel to the floor.

Another itch.

"Oh, for fuck sakes!" He reached for a hard-to-reach spot on his back to scratch, near his shoulder blades. He fidgeted and squirmed, frantically trying to reach it, and he slipped on the bloody, wet floor and hit his head on the bathroom door. "Oww!"

Now he had a bloody cut on his head.

How is it that I'm bleeding so easily? he wondered as he scratched yet another cut on his belly. It's a good thing it's a Saturday today, and I don't have to go to work.

He got out of the bathroom while scratching his left shoulder as gently as he could. He entered his bedroom and put on some shorts after ever so gently scratching his dick. Then he went into his living room scratching his right ear and turned on the TV.

He turned to the local news station hoping to find a discussion of the meteorite while scratching his right ankle. He cut himself again. The floor was bloody everywhere he'd walked on it that morning; red stains all over the living room carpet. After a few minutes, the news anchor introduced the meteorite story.

"Our correspondent, Jane Weathers, is in Potter's Field now, where the meteorite landed last night," the anchor said.

"Here we are, in Potter's Field," Weathers said, standing about ten meters in front of the meteorite, which was surrounded by men in yellow decontamination suits. "Back there is the meteorite that landed here at about 12:30 last night."

Jon leaned forward on his sofa as he watched, scratching himself on the left cheek and right hip. Yeah, he thought, scratching his right wrist. I remember hearing the thing hit the ground just after midnight.

"I have to stand this far from it because there's some kind of virus in a purple-green slime on the meteorite. It's extremely contagious," she continued.

Shaking, with his eyes agape, Jon was scratching his chest and chin, his eyes never leaving the TV screen.

"Unfortunately, a dog came by the meteorite last night, and it became infected with the virus," she went on. "The owner found the dog scratching itself to death just a few feet from the front door of her house. The dog was taken to hospital, but the doctors couldn't find any way to

remedy its sickness. The poor thing ended up dying with huge bloody gashes all over its body. In fact, the remaining, unscratched flesh just seemed to melt off. The dog is now a skeleton."

Jon was scratching his neck in a frenzy. Huge gashes of red spots were all over his body now. "Fuck me. Was that Heather's dog? She's the only dog-owner I know in this area."

"For obvious reasons, we cannot show you footage of the stages of the animal's deterioration; the visuals would be far too disturbing," the reporter said. "But we advise anyone who has been affected by the meteorite's virus to contact medical authorities and to be quarantined as soon as possible. We'll be back with more as this story develops. Jane Weathers, CXTV, Springfield."

Jon turned off the TV, then scratched a cut below his right shoulder blade. He was dripping red all over.

"I've got tiny aliens in my body," he said in a shivering voice, then scratched his left thigh, making another bloody wound. "They're eating me up. I need help. I need a doctor."

He ran out the door in a panic, scratching his sides. His neighbours' jaws dropped to see so much blood dripping from him, so many spots of red all over his body.

"Jon!" his next door neighbour said. "What the hell happened to you?" He stepped back as Jon approached.

"Whoa, whoa, whoa. Not so close, buddy. I don't wanna catch what you've got."

"Will, help me!" Jon begged with his voice cracking, him then scratching cuts on his cheeks. "I'm sick. It's the meteorite. I got too close to it, and something on it got on me."

"No offence, Jon, but stay the fuck away from me!" Will said as he continued distancing himself from Jon. He took out his cellphone. "Look, I'll call a doctor for you, OK?"

"Thanks. Aaah!" Jon screamed, falling on the ground and scratching himself all over in a desperate frenzy.

"Jesus Christ!" Will said as he watched Jon going crazy scratching more and more gashes on himself.

Other neighbours were gasping and screaming at the bloody sight. They crowded around him in a circle but didn't get too close.

One scratch that Jon gave his belly tore off a big enough chunk of skin to reveal a few inches of intestine. His blood splattered all over the ground; a bit of the intestine was hanging out of the hole.

"Cool!" a ten-year-old boy said, smiling at the fascinating gore. "Guys come here. Jon Everman's guts are showing!" The boy's friends ran over to see, pushing their way past the circle of onlookers already around Jon.

"Help...me!" he said in a hoarse voice, scratching his head and tearing off a small chunk of hair just above his right ear.

"Mom," that boy called behind him. "Can I borrow your cellphone for a minute? I wanna get some video of this freak here for show-and-tell next week."

His mom approached. "What do you want to get vi— Oh, my God!" "Your cellphone, please, Mom?" he said.

"You want to get video of that?" she said. "I don't think so."

"Oh, Mom," he said. "You're a drag!"

"You're morbid!" she said.

"Aaaah!" Jon screamed, scratching his right index finger so hard, some bone was showing. His blood sprayed everywhere.

"Holy fuck!" Will said, ducking away from the spray of red. "I just called the hospital, Jon. They should be here in a few minutes."

Jon screamed again, scratching his left cheek and tearing it off to reveal his side teeth.

"Dude stop scratching! Will said, trying to pull Jon's hands away from his neck, where he 'd just scratched a deep hole, showing off some internal neck muscle there. "You're killing yourself." A fountain of blood was gushing out.

"Don't touch me, Will!" Jon shouted, swatting Will's hand away. "You'll get the aliens on you."

Will shook all over from that swat and from the shock of Jon's tearing away of yet more outer flesh, this time from his upper left arm. Will stopped shaking after a few seconds. "Aliens? What the hell's wrong with you? Are you going mentally ill as well as physically?"

"Aliens...from the meteorite...are all over me," Jon groaned. "Aaah!" He scratched his chest, tearing off the flesh there and revealing some of his rib cage.

Everyone watching heard the wail of a siren and turned around as it got louder and closer. An ambulance arrived. It parked a few feet away from Jon and its doors were opened.

"Look at all that blood," the mother of that boy said as she and others from the circle of people surrounding

Jon made way for the EMTs. "Why hasn't he died from his wounds yet?"

A female EMT in a decontamination suit came into the circle and squatted next to Jon.

"Because there's something in the microorganisms that are keeping him alive in spite of the severity of his wounds," the EMT said. "Keep away from him, everybody; what he has is extremely contagious."

"How do the microorganisms keep him alive?' the boy's mother asked. "Why would they keep him alive?"

"We don't know for sure," the EMT said while getting her bandages ready. "They seem to feed off of whatever host they get into, be it that dog you may have heard about on the news, or this man here. Maybe keeping him alive is what keeps his body nutritious for them—I don't know." She looked down at Jon. "What's your name, sir?"

"Jon Everman," he grunted while scratching off another tuft of hair from the back of his head. "Unh!"

"Don't scratch, Jon," she said while putting a bandage on his chest. "I know it's driving you crazy, but scratching is only gonna make it worse." She hurried to get other bandages ready. "The itching is...unbearable!" he screamed, pulling his hands out of her grip so he could scratch again. "It's driving...me fucking...nuts!" He scratched his right nipple off.

"Why is his body peeling off like that?" Will asked.

"We think it's an effect of the microorganisms feeding off of him," the EMT said, still trying to restrain Jon while two other EMTs picked him up and put him on a stretcher. "Let go...of my hands!" Jon shouted.

"I'm sorry, Jon," she said. "We can't let you...scratch yourself."

"God!" he screamed.

"I know this is hard for you," she said while putting another bandage on him. "But it's for...your own good."

"How do you know the peeling is from microorganisms feeding off him?" Will asked. "Yeah," the boy's mother said. "What makes you think it's that?"

"We've been running tests of the microorganisms on lab rats," the female EMT said

while finishing putting yet another bandage on him. "We saw the scratching, the tearing off of flesh, even the flesh falling off." She got in the ambulance.

Jon was next to go in the ambulance. His arms were strapped to his sides, as were his legs, to stop him from scratching himself anymore. He shook violently and screamed, loud enough that everyone outside could hear him after the door closed.

"Good luck, Jon," Will said just before the ambulance drove away. "I'll come see you in the hospital later on."

*****

In a quarantined hospital room, screaming Jon struggled to scratch himself as soon as the

orderlies—in decontamination suits, just as were all the other staff dealing with him—removed the straps from his arms and legs. With one aggressive scratch he was able to make before the orderlies restrained him, Jon tore off a huge chunk of flesh from his upper right leg, just under his thigh. More internal muscle was showing, with blood splashing everywhere.

"Holy shit!" one of the orderlies shouted at the sight of the river of blood flowing on the sheets. "Get us some bandages!" he shouted to a nurse just outside the doorway.

The orderlies struggled to get him on his bed, holding his arms and legs to prevent more scratching. They strapped his arms and legs to the bed, a nurse came in the room to bandage his

leg, and a doctor entered after her. Jon's fidgeting made it difficult to put the bandage on; the orderlies fought to keep him still.

"Give him a sedative," the doctor told the nurse.

Once the bandage was properly put on, she stuck a needle in his arm as the doctor and the orderlies held him still. Jon calmed right down in short order. Overwhelmed with exhaustion, he passed out.

"Whew," the doctor said. "Now all we have to do is figure out how to get the alien microorganisms out of his body before they turn his skin into mashed potatoes, the way they did to that dog and those lab rats."

As Jon lay on that hospital bed, doctors in a lab on the other side of the hospital spent hours experimenting with ways to get the microorganisms out of their infected lab rats, or to kill them.

"We've had no success at all," one of them said to the doctor treating Jon. "We've tried everything. It's useless. I actually feel bad for the rats. Exposing them to the microorganisms has been nothing short of sadistic, given the hopelessness of the situation, and their obvious suffering."

"I feel even sorrier for Jon," his doctor said, then left the lab.

Several hours after Jon had fallen asleep, a nurse went into his room with a tray of food. She put it on his bedside table. He woke but closed his eyes as if to want to resume sleeping. She gave him a shot of Toradol. He budged a bit from the sting of the needle.

Then she lay a napkin on his chest and neck, stabbed a piece of meat with the fork, and brought it to his mouth.

He opened his eyes slightly.

He looked at her with a permanent frown.

"How about some food, Mr. Everman?" she said with a kind smile. "You must be really

hungry after that long sleep."

He wouldn't open his mouth. He looked almost catatonic.

"Come on," she said, still smiling. "You have to eat something."

He still wouldn't move his mouth; it wouldn't budge a millimetre.

"Come, come," she said, trying to push the meat against his lips and gently prod them

open. She then tried to push his lower lip down with her finger, but as soon as the glove of her decontamination suit touched his mouth, all the skin from his lower lip to his chin fell off, revealing his lower teeth and the middle part of his lower jaw, showing his chin bone. Blood flowed all over his neck.

"Aaaah!" she screamed, a piercing scream that rattled his ear drums so much, his ears fell off, making her scream even louder. Blood poured out from both sides in miniature cascades.

The doctor and orderlies raced into the room. The nurse fell back onto the floor. The doctor took out his penlight and brought it up to Jon's right eye.

Again, as soon as the glove of the doctor's decontamination suit touched Jon's lower eyelid to open it...

...Jon's eyeball fell out. More blood.

"Jesus!" one of the orderlies said.

Now, instead of screaming, Jon was moaning.

"Why is he only moaning?" she asked, still shaking. "The Toradol shouldn't be taking effect so soon; I only just gave him the shot now. You'd think he'd be screaming from the pain."

"The life is draining out of him," the doctor said. "He hasn't got the energy to scream."

With his remaining eye, he saw the skin from his lower jaw on his chest. Then he looked down to his left, and saw his ear lying by his shoulder. And all that blood of his...

His enervation kept him from violently jerking his body to each shocking loss of a body part, but seeing his dismembered ear was enough to make him moan louder and open that eye wider...and it fell out of its socket, too.

"Oh, my God!" another orderly said.

Jon was moaning louder and louder, moving his head from right to left. The skin on his head was loosening.

"It's too late," the doctor said with a frown of pity. "This is the end for him."

"There must be something we can for for him," the nurse sobbed. "We can't just give up on the poor guy."

"There's nothing we can do, I'm afraid," the doctor said. "All the tests we've done on the lab rats—they haven't given us the slightest clue as to how to help him."

"Oh, this is awful," she sobbed.

"Hey," the doctor said. "Be thankful that at least, to our knowledge, no one else has been infected."

Jon moaned more and more as the skin on his face was peeling off, revealing his skull.

"Can he hear what you said, Doc?" the first orderly asked. "Making him feel that all is lost will just make him hurt all the more."

"Him hearing what I said will depend on whether or not his eardrums have withered away yet." He put his penlight near Jon's ear, careful not to touch it. "It's hard to tell for sure, with all that blood in the way. Everything looks outright deformed in there. I'd say they've withered away by now."

While more and more of his skin peeled off, Jon kept moving and groaning.

"How can he still be alive?" the second orderly asked.

"We believe it's the alien microorganisms that are holding off his death, from some

special ability they have, some technology, or something, that we don't understand," the doctor said. "They're preserving him, so he'll nourish them. At least that's what we think. In any case, his death won't be much longer now. He'll be out of his misery soon enough. Then he'll have peace of mind."

The nurse just watched and sobbed.

Jon's fidgeting and rubbing his head against his pillow caused his hair and scalp—layer by layer—to fall off. His head was just a bloody skull housing a brain and tongue now.

"I can't take any more of this," the nurse said. She retched, then ran out of the room crying.

Jon's skin was melting—or so it looked—off his arms, revealing muscle and sinew. Then the muscle and sinew melted off, revealing bone. His blood was everywhere.

Please, God, don't let anyone else be afflicted with this horrible disease, the doctor thought. Neither human nor animal, for pity's sake.

Jon's jaw fell open as his head jerked forward, his chin-bone now touching his chest. His tongue and uvula fell out and landed on his chest. Then his gums melted away. He spat blood.

A sound, loud like that of blown flatulence, came from under the sheet. One of the orderlies pulled it away: Jon's exposed lungs, stomach, liver, and intestines were melting away, for the outer skin had already mostly dissolved. His heart and kidneys rolled off the bed and onto the floor; the doctor and orderlies had to dodge out of their way. That the sound of the decomposing was like blown flatulence was appropriate, for the stench was overpowering.

"It's just as what happened to the dog and lab rats," the doctor said, wincing and holding his nose, as were the others.

Jon's brain melted through his eye sockets; it poured out like beige porridge. What was left of him finally stopped moving. His blood bathed the whole bed, and a lake of red was growing all over the surrounding floor. One of the orderlies put a sheet over the skeleton.

*****

Will arrived at the hospital about an hour later. When he saw staff in decontamination suits going down the hall, he correctly assumed they were dealing with Jon. His doctor was among them.

"Hey, doctor," he called out to them. The doctor turned and looked at him. "Do you know how Jon Everman is doing?"

"Are you one of his family?" the doctor asked with a frown.

"No," Will said. "I'm his neighbour. I'd just like to know what happened to him."

The doctor took a deep breath and said, "I'm afraid he didn't make it. Like the dog, if you heard the news story about it; your neighbour is just a skeleton now."

"Well, I had a feeling it would turn out that way," Will said, scratching his eyebrow.

"Thanks."

"Wish I could have done better," the doctor said. "Now if you'll excuse me, I have a lot of work to do." Then he walked away.

"I'll bet you do," Will said, scratching his shoulder.

No Man Left Behind

Scott M. Goriscak

I was eating my breakfast in the mess tent when the thunder of bombs detonating north of our camp startled me. I looked in the direction of the explosions and saw plumes of smoke column upward into the sky. Within moments of the bombing our advanced reconnaissance team radioed in. They were observing the village that was our next target to drive out terrorist elements. The initial report stated that the village was under attack. My question was, by whom? The scout reported a group of unfriendlies shelling and launching an assortment of missiles and jet-propelled grenades on the opposite side of the village. Apparently the cruel, self-appointed dictator had sent his troops to instill fear of his wrath among the villagers, to inspire them to take up arms against our advancing forces and to deter them from surrendering and retreating; but his soldiers missed their target and instead of scaring the villagers bombed the village!

The number of reported village casualties grew as the missiles rained over the area. The last few missiles exploded on impact and a haze of red powder spewed into the air. The slow descent of the mysterious residue covered everyone and everything in its path. Chaos defined the townspeople's panicked reaction to the destruction around them. A closer look through the scout's binoculars revealed massive bleeding from the defenseless population's eyes and ears. They ran blindly into one another and into the walls of the buildings. The unknown agent had robbed them of their sight. The next heart-wrenching radio message reported that the affected population were dying in the streets as the red cloud began to settle. Then the wind gave the deadly dust new life as it lifted it into the air!

The scout continued to radio in "Red cloud seems to be spreading in the wind. It's turning in our ..." The communication ceased mid sentence! The next message was muffled and incoherent. We could only assume that the team had to suit up and the radioman was trying to speak through his chemical mask. We asked him to repeat his message when what he was attempting to convey became apparent!

The blaring of the camp's chemical alarms warned us of what the radioman was probably attempting to communicate: an impending chemical contamination. I grabbed for my atropine injection from my leg pocket. I popped its cap open and stabbed it hard into the thigh muscle of my right leg. There was no time to run to my tent and dress in my chemical suit as I felt the desert wind blow against my face. I prayed that the airborne agent wouldn't cause a painful death from infected blisters. I watched nervously as the colors of the litmus patches of my uniform reacted confirming that I had been exposed to a chemical agent. Knowing that death was all around us, I was as mentally prepared as anyone could be. I hoped that if I were going to die it would be quick and painless. I glanced down at my uniform. The strange colors of the litmus patches identified an unfamiliar chemical and puzzled me. Not knowing what I had been exposed to I continued to wait for the expected ill effects of exposure—blistering, burning, airway constriction— but none came. When the alarms went silent signaling the air was safe, the commander gave the order to begin decontamination. One by one each man walked through the tent and was sprayed with a chemical to decontaminate him and his gear.

After an hour of cleansing our equipment and the campgrounds of any harmful trace of the mysterious chemical, the members of the squadron returned to their normal duties preparing for the night's surge into the village ahead.

At approximately 15:00 the ghastly effects of the morning's missile attacks revealed their horrid aftermath. The radio reports resumed from the recon team to the commander.

"Alpha base 1."

"This is alpha base. Over."

"Scout 1 reporting. Family of fallen villagers have come to claim the dead. Wait! Commander! The villagers are attacking!"

"Who are the villagers attacking?"

"The villagers killed by the bombing are getting up and attacking the people that came to help them! They are eating them!" The commander asked him to repeat his last transmission.

"The dead villagers are eating the living! Repeat. The presumed dead villagers are up and walking around! They are eating anything that is alive!"

The commander asked for the scout to repeat his report, thinking that their communication had been distorted in transmission.

The grisly details continued to unfold as the newly resurrected victims fed. The radioman started to cry as he witnessed the emaciated dead devour a group of terrified young school children! After the children were all gone the dead moved on to the elderly. When all human life had been exterminated at the hands of the already dead, they turned and looked in the direction of the recon team. The communications officer continued to narrate the gruesome details to base camp as the army walked in their direction.

Communication of the morbid details continued for the next hour and then the radio signal abruptly ended. Our radioman continued to try to re-establish communications with the recon team without success. In a brief moment we heard the signal re-establish and the sounds of gunfire reverberated through the radio before falling silent again. The commander asked for air support from headquarters. Minutes later two A-10 tank killer aircrafts flew over the base toward the recon team's last coordinates. The commander ordered them to locate and provide support to the team on the ground, then waited patiently for news.

Then the pilot came over the air. "Located your team surrounded by unfriendlies. All deceased! Permission to engage? Over."

Without hesitation the commander gave the order for lethal action. The sound of exploding ordnance was followed by aircraft gun fire. After numerous fly-bys the pilots riddled the landscape with munitions. Confident their mission was complete the pilot radioed in, "Enemy terminated."

The pilot circled while the smoke cleared and then reported, "Negative, enemy is still advancing."

"Advancing where?" the commander barked.

"Advancing in your direction. Over."

The commander paused then spoke into the radio, "Continue with bombing run and target all weaponry."

The pilot replied, "No weapons present."

The commander again unsure of what he had just heard asked the pilot to repeat his message.

"Advancing unfriendlies unarmed. I repeat, unarmed."

The commander asked the pilot how they could defeat a fully armed squadron.

Pilot response, "Overtook by force of numbers."

"Continue assault until you exhaust all munitions. Over," the commander ordered.

"Affirmative." The pilot radioed back.

The commander raised the camp's alert level. Every man was to pick up a rifle and stand a post. The pilots radioed in that they enemy was still approaching, and they were forced to return to the airstrip for re-armament and refueling. They would return within the hour as we dug in and readied ourselves for the enemy. The EOD squadron lined the dunes between us and the approaching enemy with Claymore Mines. An explosion from these would obliterate all life for fifty yards. Bomb run after bomb run the fighter jets failed to keep the enemy from reaching our front door.

Darkness had fallen and we all waited to engage the enemy. We knew the jets and their efforts were failing to stop the advancing enemy as their bombs dropped nearer to our camp with each run. The moon was low in the sky illuminating the silhouettes of the enemy as they emerged over the dunes in the distance. Some of the men began to shoot prematurely as their fright prompted them, but the commander halted their assault.

Where are they all coming from? I asked myself. They kept advancing and the pilots were correct--they weren't fighting back! The pilots radioed in that they were out of ammunition and running low on fuel. They broke off their attack and were returning to their air strip, which left us without air support, on our own. I turned to ask the commander for his orders, and he was gone! I looked around and thought I caught a glimpse of him running in the opposite direction of the enemy. He was going AWOL!

His decision to abandon his troops forced me into a leadership position. I was the next highest-ranking officer and the men all looked to me for our next move. I found myself burdened with a difficult decision. I ordered them to fire at will. The night was punctuated by the bright arcs of tracer rounds as they raced across the void, striking the darkened enemy as they approached, but without harming effects. Enemy numbers kept growing until there must have been around three hundred.

Where are they all coming from? I asked myself again.

After a half hour we had exhausted our stockpile of ammunition and the enemy kept advancing on us. Now I wrestled with the burden of upholding the rules of engagement created by the Geneva Convention and the United Nations and let my men be slaughtered or choosing to violate them and save my men. I decided that I had no choice but to ignore the rules and attempt to save our lives. I ordered the men to suit up in their chemical suits and masks. I instructed the tanks and artillery to load their weapons with the WMD munitions we had confiscated from our previous enemy raids. They all looked oddly at my request, but the sight on the oncoming enemy quickly provoked them. I ordered them to fire when ready.

The bombs started exploding and I prayed that the poisonous gases we were utilizing in our counterattack would put an end to the madness. We continued firing the shells and mortars until we exhausted even the illegal weaponry. When the gaseous cloud dissipated all that remained were the gaunt silhouettes of the army of the dead advancing over the top of the dunes. I had done the unthinkable to defeat my adversaries, only to fail. All that remained between us and the walking dead were the

Claymores! Without hesitation I gave the order to detonate!

The Claymores' exploding force eradicated the landscape along with the oncoming army. We had done it! We had defeated the army! The men cheered as they witnessed the destruction of their foes. Then the smoke cleared, and reality revealed to us how short-lived our victory was. Within moments mutilated Claymore victims rained down on us. Many of my men were in various stages of undress from their protective chemical suits when deadly-chemical-laced heads, limbs, and assorted body parts fell from the sky. Men started collapsing from the direct contact with the toxic body parts. But this wasn't the worst revelation. I looked on in wild amazement as the disturbing scene unfolded before me. The dismembered body parts began moving of their own accord! Decapitated heads bounced and rolled toward the troops! Severed fingers and toes landed on or near the men, inch-worming and boring their way into various orifices of soldier's bodies, cruelly and slowly killing them. The sight of the arms and legs squirming along the sand in search of other victims distracted me long enough for an infected, severed upper torso to crawl out of the dark shades of the night, grab hold of my leg, and bite into it! I collapsed to the ground as the pain pulsed from the wound. I attempted to shake the intruder from my leg without success. I drew my firearm, aimed it, and fired my last round! The bullet extracted the left eye from its socket and blew a hole through the back of the skull, but the head remained attached to me. I discarded my gun and tried to pry it off with my bare hands but only managed to tear its nose from its face. I grabbed at its ears and they came off, too. The head tightened its jaws, severing a chunk of muscle from my leg through my pants leg. I didn't understand how something so fragile could be such a formidable adversary. I grasped the handle of my knife and pulled it from its sheath. I slid the serrated blade across the throat of my attacker sawing through it till the head released and fell to the sand before resuming its rolling attack, narrowly missing me as I limped away.

I didn't know what to do. What was left? Not sure I was capable of rational thought with the hideous chaos going on all around me; I came up with the solution: gas! I quickly screamed out to the men to retreat, instructing them to search out fuel and flammables from around the camp. Twenty men set out in search of the fuel; only five of us returned. I ordered the remaining men to douse anything that moved with the flammables and regroup at the rear gate of the camp.

Having completed the assigned task, the men regrouped with me as instructed. I pulled a flare gun from my pack and aimed it at what was left of the base camp. In the darkness of the night the sand looked alive as the wave of fuel-soaked body parts converged upon us. I fired the flare gun igniting the camp into a gigantic fireball! The wildly animated body parts began to cook, suffocating us with the sickly aroma of burning flesh. Flaming body parts crawled or rolled from the fire and died as the life was barbecued from them. After all was done only five of us survived the night of horror.

We walked all night until the sunrise greeted us over the horizon. In the morning light I looked back at our camp smoldering in the distance. Ahead of us I could see the outline of a single structure remaining in our previous camp where I hoped to find some supplies from our prior occupation. The further we walked the more my wounded leg throbbed in pain. Our uniforms were so blood-splattered from the night's battle that it camouflaged my wound. When we reached the camp, we searched for any supplies that we might have left behind. We were fortunate to discover a backpack of MRE's and a few precious rounds of ammunition. I divided the MREs among us equally. The men were hungry. I thought I was, too, but when I tried to eat, I was repulsed by the food. I didn't understand why; I was starving. I kept trying to force myself to eat, but when I finally succeeded to get a mouthful down my stomach refused it and I vomited.

After settling in and ascertaining that the threat we left behind the night before wasn't tracking us, we set up our camp and prepared it for living and defending if need be. We scheduled a rotating sleep shift and guard shift. At about five o'clock while I was walking guard duty, I started to feel odd. I was scratching an itch on my arm when my fingernail peeled away. I looked at the others and I pulled at my thumbnail; it fell away, too! What is going on? I thought. The sensation was surreal, but surprisingly painless. I heard footsteps from behind. The soldier was here to relieve me of my guard duty, and I needed some sleep. I don't know why I felt the need to conceal my affliction, but I quickly stuffed my hand into my pocket. I walked back to my backpack and unrolled my sleeping tarp and blanket to protect myself from the cold desert night.

It was still dark when I awoke by an irritated itch on the side of my head. I sat up and reached up to scratch my head. Something was very wrong! I stopped scratching and placed my hand flat against it. My ear was missing! I looked down and saw it resting on my blanket. I reached for the other ear. I was relieved that it was still there, but only temporarily—it fell from my head as my fingers touched it. What was happening to me? Then I recalled the hideous head that bit me. I remembered the tenacity of its frail features as I fought with it. It infected me and I was transforming into whatever it had been. I was scared. I lay back down and contemplated what to do next.

I awoke to the rat-a-tat-tat of gunfire! I scrambled to my feet and felt the queer changes in my body as I tried to maintain my balance. I grabbed my helmet in an attempt to conceal my earless head and without checking, in fear that I might dislodge another body part, I stumbled toward the commotion. I made my way around the corner of the building expecting to see the return of the enemy combatants. The unfolding scene was disturbing. The sergeant of our squadron—or what I thought was the sergeant—was sitting, gaunt and pallid, over one of the men. His eyes were gloomy and dead. His infection was stages ahead of mine. He had killed the private on guard duty and sat above his victim rapaciously slurping and sifting through the bloody innards and organs as he ate. The scene was so unnerving to me knowing that this was my certain demise.

I was so angry at my affliction that I took it out on the walking corpse. I pulled out my pistol and fired at the hideous figure. The bullet struck him in the shoulder. Unfazed, he growled at me and then resumed voraciously devouring his quarry. The other two men, sickened by the sight, followed my example and fired their sidearms until they were empty. Bullets struck the empty-eyed NCO in the chest and the head. The creature paused, his eyes rolled back in his head as he began to sway back and forth before falling dead over his victim. Or so we hoped. We pulled the atrocity from our fallen comrade. How could this have happened? Two good men, lost.

I began to feel queasy, and I wasn't the only one. I watched as one of the other men became ill emptying the contents of his stomach into the sand. I told them that I would be right back; I needed to get some fresh air. I walked back around the building, then without warning a mask of uncertainty came over my thoughts. The feeling was followed by increased fatigue and loss of memory. I struggled to control my thoughts and actions until I no longer cared. I could hear senseless utterances coming from my mouth until I lost the ability to speak. All that remained was predatory hunger. I needed to eat. Now!

I felt myself walking toward the men, as if I were a marionette under someone else's control. I needed food! I emerged from the cover of the building to find only one of the men present. His back was turned to me as he dug a hole to bury the dead. He heard me coming and said something to me, but I could no longer understand his words. With no response from me he turned to face me, and I plunged my knife into his chest. He looked at me with a horrible mask of disbelief as his knees buckled and he silently fell to the ground before me. I could feel my cravings heighten as I smelled the blood from his wound. I bit into his face and tore away a mouthful of flesh with my teeth. I chewed the rubbery mass before swallowing hard. I continued to gnaw, sometimes swallowing without chewing. I fed until I was satisfied, rendering my victim faceless. The other two men returned to find me as I was finishing my meal. Horror gripped their faces as they looked down at me. They drew their weapons and fired. The only sound that could be heard was the click of their empty guns. They both ran away knowing they were defenseless against me without their weapons.

I pursued them, helpless to control my own actions. This inner craving drove my decaying shell to hunt and feed. I took in the dry desert air in search of the soldier's scent. The swirling desert wind camouflaged their location. I walked around the building and saw one of the men in the distance as he fled the scene. I entered the bombed-out ruins of the building in pursuit of my next meal. Then the faint sound of muffled voices caught my attention through the rushing silence of the building. I reached the radioman just as he was relaying his co-ordinates for an air strike. The voice on the radio confirmed the information and the order. He looked up just as I walked around the debris that had concealed him. He yanked the wire and the mic from the transmitter to protect his orders from being rescinded.

I bent down and grabbed a large stone and raised it over my head. In response he could do nothing but scream. I slammed the stone down into his head. I rendered him unconscious with the first blow. The blood spilled down over his face, but I was unsatisfied. I wanted more; I wanted to eat. I continued striking the brick into his skull until my meal was ready for consumption. I dropped the bloodied rock and sat down next to my victim. I grabbed his head and pulled at the fragments of his skull that covered the brain. Piece by piece I peeled them away till I exposed the soft gray tissue hiding below. When I was finished prepping my meal, I started to eat using his skull as a bowl pulling and scooping the gray matter from it as I gorged myself on the warm, spongy meal. I stuffed the pieces of his brain into my mouth by the handfuls. When my bowl was empty, I stood up and abandoned his corpse in search of my next meal.

I searched for the man who had fled from the base earlier. I had trouble locating him, but I caught his scent in the distance. I turned and walked in his direction. I walked only a few feet when the roar of an engine startled me. I looked up and saw the approaching aircraft followed by a parachute blooming open as it fell through the air. The object dangling in the air below the parachute was the FOH-1 explosive. The initials stood for "Fires of Hell." On impact everything within a mile would be sucked into Ground Zero and incinerated. I watched knowing I couldn't do a damned thing about it in this body. I continued in my mindless journey in search of food, aware of the impending doom descending upon me.

I underestimated the destructive capability of the explosive. The force of the blast as it impacted was far worse than I could have imagined. The force of the bomb violently tossed me to the ground. A moment later grabbed me and pulled me to the center of the fiery blast that imploded the area. As I flew through the air, I saw everything around me destroyed by the explosion. When I reached the fire, I saw its flaming fingers dancing across my body but felt nothing as the fire broiled my skin and muscle from my bones and paralyzed me.

Some time later I lay motionless, smoldering on the dessert sand, as the soldier who escaped my grasp returned with a squadron of men. He looked down at my charred remains and saluted. The only part of me that still functioned was the part that wanted to eat him. He raised his sidearm and fired the weapon into my head! I felt the bullet punch its way through my forehead then ricochet off the interior of my skull before lodging itself in my brain. The bullet stopped, but it continued to sizzle in its resting place. I waited eagerly for death, but it never came. His bullet had failed to extinguish my consciousness.

My body was dead to the world, but my blood-craving brain, alive within the walls of my skull for eternity watched as the lid of the coffin clicked in place entombing me forever in the cold darkness. I screamed for help, but all fell silent on the ears of my grieving friends and family. I was the only audience to my pleas as they echoed within the confines of my mind.

The one who enters the body

Norbert Góra

Stars, even if they wanted to,
can't announce him
like a lightning seen from afar,
he comes in filth of silence,
the one who slides from the sky
to carry the strings of the mind,
I am a doll, a mannequin, an empty hole
in which he enters like a king into the castle.

He flies through the bowels,
touching the intestine
and wraps around the heart
like an indestructible hawthorn,
strange bliss codes the waves of pain
that flow through the body
at the speed of blood.

He leaves the interior,
bored and saturated,
for a moment looking
at the work of destruction,
tears flow,
blood flows,
combined in one stream,
pain moans,
I scream,
but one thing I know
it is not a dream.

Breathing more and more
uneven,
eyes more and more
blurry,
although I am still trying
to remember how it disappears –
his face,
my life,
you ruthless creature,
goodbye.

Authors, Gunmen, and Other Strange Creatures

Andy Rausch

Paul Trimble was tired of the whole book tour thing, but his book wasn't gonna sell itself. The tour was the aspect of being a writer he hated most. He loved writing, disliked editing, and absolutely hated touring from city to city, appearing at bookstores and sleeping in bargain motels so he could hawk his book. And it wasn't just that he felt it was undignified, although he did, but it was the loneliness. It was sitting in his room each night, either drunk and alone or drunk with some young lit groupie twink. But the good thing was, his hard work was paying off. After seven weeks, The Life and Crimes of Bingo Crawford was still number nine on the New York Times bestseller list.

Paul wasn't stupid, and he wasn't gonna quit now. Not only was the book selling like meth at a Kid Rock show, but this was a problem he'd spent decades dreaming of having. When he'd been a twenty-something kid sending out half-cooked yarns and waiting by the mailbox for form rejections, he would have killed to be a successful novelist on a book tour. But Paul had learned that accomplishing one's dreams was rarely as satisfying as one envisions.

So here he was, out here touring. Where was he tonight? Philly? DC? Right, right, he thought. That was it—Washington, DC. Tonight, he would be visiting one of the last remaining mom-and-pop bookstores. It was a legendarily cool store, so at least there was that. His

106

buddy Sam Dean, a horror novelist, had told him that the store, Dead Trees, was a book-lover's dream. "They focus on actual literature," Sam had said. "They don't even sell shit like Twilight or any of that Dan Brown stuff. To tell you the truth, I'm surprised they carry my books. They're very selective about what they carry, and discerning readers travel far and wide to shop there. That's how they've managed to stay open so long." Of course, this praise had come from Sam Dean, a married man who'd slept with hundreds of women, and was far from the last word on integrity.

Despite Sam's recommendation, Paul didn't want to be here. Cool place or no, he was over it. Tonight, he told himself, he would drink, and drink to excess. It was just one of those nights, he said. Of course, every night was one of those nights now, but who was counting?

When the driver stopped in front of the store, Paul thanked him and got out, approaching the building. He made his way past the people waiting in line to see him. "Where are you going?" some guy asked. "We were here first, dickbag! Go to the end of like everybody else!" Paul smiled and told him, "I'm Paul Trimble." Paul could see from the man's expression that his name didn't ring a bell, begging the question, why was he here? But Paul was aware that people weren't buying the book for his writing. They bought it because they wanted to read stories about incarcerated crime boss Bingo Crawford. They were also buying it because a massive ad campaign had brainwashed them into doing so.

Paul stood there, staring at the man. He was momentarily unsure what to say. Before he could say the wrong thing—Paul's specialty—a bookstore employee came to his rescue.

"Thanks," he told the guy who led him in. He was a clean-cut young blonde who looked about twenty-five.

He was attractive, definitely in Paul's wheelhouse, and he wondered if he might be a queer star-fucker who liked writers. He made a mental note to investigate further after the signing.

The bookstore was massive, bigger than any mom-and-pop store Paul had ever seen. It had the perfect ambiance. It was comfortable, warm, and smelled like lattes, which Paul saw as the ideal combination. The man led him to the store's manager, a forty-something woman who looked like a less attractive Laura Linney. They shook hands and she introduced herself as Rachel before showing him around. Customers were filtering in, but there was already a substantial crowd congregated inside, waiting to hear him speak.

Paul milled around, looking at books as he waited. Finally, after awhile, Rachel led him to a microphone. She welcomed everyone and thanked them for their attendance. "Tonight, we have Mr. Paul Trimble, who is the author of the new book—" She stopped and looked at the dust jacket of the book she was carrying. "The Life and Crimes of Bingo Crawford," she said. "After he's done talking, we'll have a Q&A, and then we'll have a signing for everyone who purchases the book." She stepped aside, allowing Paul to move behind the mic.

He thanked her and looked around the room at the clapping misfits who'd come to listen. He'd spoken more than twenty times now, and it was still awkward. Some people had a gift for speaking, but Paul did not. He gave the audience some background about the book, making a few tried-and-true jokes about the writing process, and then sharing his grandmother's motto that books were always the answer and that they would always save you from any problem. The audience responded favorably, and Paul read an excerpt. His earliest readings had been far messier occasions as he'd been unsure which passage to read. But after seeing what worked and what didn't, he'd started reading a section where Bingo chops off a mobster's penis and forces him eat it. Audiences always reacted favorably, and tonight was no exception.

When it came time for the Q&A, Paul stumbled a bit when asked about fictionalized accounts of real-life events. "How do you know what the people actually said?" a middle-aged weirdo in a Chewbacca shirt and fedora asked. Paul had no problem with the question, and felt it was valid, but stuttered in his response, and then somehow wandered into the weeds, talking about something else altogether.

Things became interesting when a guy in the front row asked, "Do you know what Bingo Crawford thinks about the book?" The man continued standing as Paul explained he'd heard nothing regarding Crawford's opinion, but said he was sure Crawford knew of its existence. "I doubt he'd have any problem with my book since all of these events have been detailed previously in non-fiction books." He looked at the man as he wrapped up his response, and the man moved forward, coming towards him. Paul didn't realize what was happening until he saw the chrome pistol coming up from beside him. The man leveled the gun at him. Paul stood there, his eyes huge, and time stopped.

"Mr. Crawford didn't care for your book," said the man. "He sends his regards."

This was the moment Paul knew he would die. He saw the man tense up, his finger pulling the trigger. Paul closed his eyes instinctively, as if this would stop it.

It was then he heard the deafening sound of the plate-glass window shattering. Paul turned his head towards the sound, his eyes open, and saw a monstrous creature in the window. In this second, people began screaming, and the gunman fired wildly, his bullet zipping into the wall behind Paul. People were screaming and pushing one another, crowding together and falling over each other, and suddenly there were people between Paul and the gunman.

Then the creature screeched loudly, perhaps as introduction. Paul looked at it, a great monstrosity unlike anything he'd ever seen or imagined. It had wings, extended, brown like its body, that were so long they could barely fit within the frame of the window. It dragged itself in, its appearance grotesque. It wrecked everything it encountered, either crushing it beneath its feet or demolishing it with its thrashing spiked tail. It had tiny T-rex arms, unlike any arms Paul had ever seen; they wiggled fluidly as if they had no bones. The creature's ghastly head, pointed and hairy, resembling a rat's, was somehow enveloped in flames, like Ghost Rider's skull.

The creature's arms flailed, and it screeched a loud, piercing cry that made Paul's blood curdle. Everyone was stumbling over one another, crowding towards the back of the room. The creature moved forward, knocking over racks and tables, its thrashing tail obliterating everything in its wake. Between the screeching creature and the attendants' screams and gasps, Dead Trees was now filled with perpetual sound.

Any other time, Paul would have wondered what the creature was and where it had come from, but this was a unique situation. He turned to run, but there was nowhere to go. And there was the gunman to be considered. Paul turned towards him, seeing him standing there engulfed in a sea of people, still staring at him with a look that said he was going to kill him. This fucker was persistent, unmoved by the creature's presence.

There was no visible exit at the back of the room, and the creature stood between Paul and the front entrance. What could he do? As he stared at the gunman, he saw him extend his arm towards him. The gun was up and out. Paul turned and shoved his way forward just as it fired, its shot somehow managing to pierce the cacophony. He heard a man behind him scream out in pain, but Paul continued moving.

He wondered if people were reacting to the gunman, maybe even trying to take the gun, but he couldn't stop to look. He pushed his way through the crowd, shoving people to get through, making his way towards the creature. The creature continued to screech wildly. Paul heard another gunshot, but this one was ahead and to his right. He straightened himself, looking over the crowd. He saw a man, older, maybe seventy, with a pistol aimed at the creature. The creature was reacting as if it had been shot, but Paul saw no blood. The man was standing before the beast, out in front of the other people who were pushing in the opposite direction, and he fired a second shot. His shot struck the thing point blank in its chest, right between its tiny arms, and it screeched again, but it didn't bleed.

Suddenly the creature leaped towards him, and it was on the man, its head snapping forward, catching the man's head in its teeth. The man attempted to break free, but to no avail. The creature leaned back, lifting the man's flailing torso. It chomped down hard, and the man's headless body fell limp to the floor. Paul looked at the creature, saw it chewing the man's head, and then it finished and resumed crashing forward.

Paul was fucked, and he knew it. He looked back in the direction of the gunman but couldn't see him. He had to move, or the gunman would catch him. Paul wasn't like the creature; he wasn't bulletproof. So, he pushed through the crowd, finally reaching its edge, and made his way into the space between the crowd and the creature. The creature stared at him, perhaps sizing him up, but Paul guessed it was just a dumb beast with no means to question or decipher motives.

The creature's eyes were locked on him. He moved towards the creature, and it stood motionless, just staring, perhaps confused.

"I've got you, you fucker!" came a voice from Paul's right. He turned towards it, already knowing who it was. He saw the gunman moving out of the crowd, maybe fifteen feet away. The gunman had his pistol trained on Paul, and he was grinning, somehow oblivious to all this.

"Why?" cried Paul.

"Mr. Crawford says so," said the man. "That's all either of us needs to know."

Paul started to respond, but the creature was suddenly on the gunman. In his final seconds, the gunman realized what was happening. He turned towards the creature, just in time to see its open mouth chomping down around his head. And the gunman was gone, now a headless body toppling to the floor.

Seeing the creature distracted and eating, Paul broke into a sprint, hoping to run to its left, making his way out before it knew what was happening. Paul was about three steps into his run when the creature turned its head. The gunman's skull was in its mouth, its teeth still grinding, but the creature managed a garbled screech.

Paul was running, and the creature moved towards him, maybe ten feet away now. Paul knew it would block his path, so he panicked. He didn't know what to do, so he grabbed a book from a display and threw it wildly in the direction of the creature. The book struck the creature in its face and it reared back in shock. Paul stumbled towards the window, grabbing a second book. He stopped long enough to hurl it, striking the creature in the side of its head. The creature stepped back, wobbling now. Was it in pain? Paul knew something was askew. He should have been running, but he stopped, staring at the thing. The creature just stood there, its head facing the floor.

Paul heard the sound and realized what was happening: the creature was choking on the gunman's head. It stood there, swaying, shaking its head, continuing to choke, unable to dislodge the half-chewed remains from its throat. It continued to struggle, its head shaking wildly, making the choking sound. Then, suddenly, it fell over, thrashing wildly, knocking over a giant book display. This continued for another thirty seconds, and then, finally, the creature went still, apparently dead. The flames surrounding the creature's head now spread onto the carpet, which caught fire.

Paul stood there watching the flames spread, considering how his throwing the book had stunned the creature, causing it to choke. He thought it humorous that the creature was impervious to bullets but wound up being stopped by a Chuck Palahniuk book. Paul reflected on his grandmother's words about how books were always the answer and that books would always save you. She was right, he thought. A book had saved him.

He moved towards the broken window, stepping out to freedom.

He needed a drink.

But this thought was interrupted when he was rammed by a charging wolf creature with horns. It pierced Paul with its horns, causing him to fall hard to the pavement. Before he could react, the creature bit into his neck. There was blood everywhere, and the pain was immense. It was sharp and searing, but it was short-lived. The sight of the creature covered in blood and gnawing at his neck was the last thing Paul would ever see. And then there was darkness. The sight of the creature covered in blood and gnawing at his neck was the last thing Paul would see.

Maggona Beach

David B. Harrington

In May of 1970, while everybody was singing and dancing to Octopus's Garden, I waltzed into the Museum of Natural History and was immediately escorted to a waiting room on the second floor. The nameplate on the office door to my left read: Dr. Fredrick Stephens, Marine Biologist & Director of Ichthyology, and I knew I was in the right place. I had been summoned by Dr. Stephens just days earlier regarding the possible discovery of a new species of Periophthalmus in the mangrove swamps of southern India.

A few moments later the door swung open and out stepped a distinguished, rather portly gentleman in his mid-fifties with a full beard and mustache, wearing horn-rimmed spectacles and a white lab coat. I stood up to introduce myself and graciously extended my hand. "You must be Doctor Stephens?" I said politely.

"Yes. And you must be Peter. Thanks for dropping by, I've been expecting you. Won't you come in please?" His office was surprisingly small and cramped, his desk cluttered with stacks of textbooks and scientific journals. "Pardon the mess," he said apologetically as he cleared a spot for me to sit. "Things have been rather chaotic around here lately. Please, won't you sit down?"

"Thank you very much."

"Professor Khandir tells me you are quite the adventurer…?" He squinted and scrutinized me for a moment before continuing. "I'm afraid I am a little pressed for time, so let's get right down to business, shall we? A couple of weeks ago I received word that a former associate and dear friend of mine accidentally fell overboard and drowned while on a scuba diving expedition in the Indian Ocean."

"Oh goodness gracious! How unfortunate. My sincere condolences, sir."

"Yes. Thank you, Peter. He will be sorely missed I assure you. The captain of the diving team claims that Calvin had been acting rather peculiar and even seemed a bit delusional in the hours leading up to his death." Dr Stephens rolled his chair over to an old metal file cabinet, produced a set of keys from his coat pocket, and unlocked one of the drawers. He pulled out a manila envelope and handed it to me, "Evidently the night before his tragic accident he also drew these sketches. Take a look at them and tell me what you think. I'm sure you will find them quite interesting. The good captain said Calvin was raving like a lunatic over dinner about some strange sea creatures he had encountered on one of his earlier dives. Supposedly there were calm seas for the entire duration of the voyage. I fear that he may have deliberately taken his own life."

I opened the envelope and started thumbing through the drawings. I could not believe what I was seeing. "What in pink carnations are these things?" I said emphatically. "Are these for real?" The sketches depicted odd and dreadfully disturbing sea creatures the likes of which I have never seen before and what can only be described as cyclopean cephalopods with big bulging eyes, long tentacles, scaly tail-like appendages, and razor-sharp fangs protruding from the top of their mouths. Several of the sketches depicted dozens of these fishy creatures knotted together in a massive heap of eyeballs, teeth and tentacles.

"I'm sorry, doctor, but I'm a little confused. When we spoke on the phone the other day you said you wanted to talk to me about a new species of Periophthalmus. You didn't mention anything about these drawings."

"My apologies, Peter. I didn't mean to mislead you in any way. It's just that we're trying to keep this sensitive matter under wraps until it can be investigated further. I hope you understand?"

"Of course. But why did you contact me in the first place?"

"Well, Peter, you were highly recommended by Professor Khandir. She is quite fond of you, you know, and thought that you might like to join her in Ceylon to look into this matter. You know, poke around a bit, see what you can come up with. The museum is prepared to pay you quite handsomely. We would, of course, provide you with all the necessary paperwork, and your travel expenses would be compensated in full should you accept our offer. Accommodations have already been made." He reached into his shirt pocket and handed me a round trip airline ticket, "Your flight is scheduled for the 26th of May, which gives you five days to get ready. Professor

Khandir has made arrangements to have you picked up at the airport the following day."

"And will you be coming along too, doctor?" I inquired.

"No, I'm afraid not. This is our busiest time of the year and I have prior commitments here at the museum. We have notified the Ceylonese government about our investigation, so you can expect full cooperation from the local authorities. Oh, and Peter, as I'm sure you are aware, it is monsoon season down there, so be sure to pack extra rain gear and plenty of insect repellent. I hear the mosquitoes can get rather nasty. I think that about covers it. Do you have any questions before I let you go?"

"Yes. How long am I expected to be away?"

"Two, maybe three weeks tops. Anything else?"

"Not that I can think of."

"Good! I will arrange for a taxi to pick you up and take you to the airport. And I will get in touch with Professor Khandir tomorrow to let her know you'll be coming. She'll be absolutely delighted, I'm sure. One more thing, Peter. As an added incentive, the museum is also prepared to reward you with a substantial bonus, a finder's fee if you will, should you happen to capture one or two specimens and bring them back alive in a discreet manner."

The transatlantic plane ride from JFK to Ceylon was long and exhausting, but relatively smooth except for some minor turbulence as we passed over the north

African coastline. I had an hour layover in Bombay where the monsoon rains were coming down so hard it felt like a typhoon. The 747 jumbo jet had a bumpy take off but landed safely in Colombo right on schedule. The cab was already waiting for me outside the terminal.

I arrived at the University of Colombo at 3:30 PM, exactly twelve hours after leaving New York. The Department of Zoology was a large, modern-style facility in the heart of campus. I checked in with the receptionist first and she said Professor Khandir was expecting me. I took the elevator down to the basement and found her in the Marine Sciences Lab tending to her mudskippers just as I knew she would be. She didn't notice me come in, so I stood at the doorway and watched her for a minute or two. I first met Professor Agneya Khandir, or 'Aggie' as everybody called her, in Gambia a couple of years earlier and was immediately taken by her good looks. She was a Ceylonese beauty in her mid-thirties with jet black hair, deep wine dark eyes, and a gorgeous hourglass figure. She could have easily been an exotic Indonesian princess, but she was an island girl through and through and I admired her greatly. I set my bags down, "Ahem."

She got all excited when she saw me and came running over to give me an affectionate hug. I squeezed her tight. Ah! The sweet fragrance of cinnamon and citrus fruit was intoxicating. "Peter! There you are, darling. I'm so glad you made it. It's good to see you again."

"It's wonderful to see you again too, Aggie! You're looking fabulous as always."

"Aw, shucks. You're so sweet." She gave me a once over, "You're not looking so bad yourself. Thanks for coming all this way."

"My pleasure! I'm really looking forward to our little adventure in this tropical paradise of yours."

"Come over here! I want to introduce you to our latest newlyweds." I followed her over to a five hundred-gallon paludarium filled with mudskippers, or 'blennies' as she liked to call them. "Aren't they adorable? I even named one after you, Peter."

"I'm flattered. You really shouldn't have."

"He reminds me of you. Always chasing the female around," she chortled.

"Real funny, professor," I remarked jokingly.

"Well, I'm sure we'll see a lot more tomorrow."

"I'm sure we will. So where exactly are we going anyway?"

"To a place just down the coast called Maggona Beach. It's only about an hour's drive from here. We'll be lodging at a cozy little bungalow called the Paladin Inn."

"Ooh! Sounds romantic."

She smiled and said, "Now who's being funny? Tomorrow morning we'll go down to the mudflats and have a look around to see if we can find anything unusual. I presume Dr. Stephens showed you the drawings?"

"As a matter of fact, he did. I'm still trying to wrap my head around it. He seems convinced that those creatures of his really are out there. They don't resemble anything I've ever seen before, that's for sure. What do you make of them, Aggie?"

"To tell you the truth, I'm a little skeptical about the whole idea myself. I just hope he's not sending us off on some kind of wild goose chase."

"Me either," I agreed.

"So, yeah, it looks like it's just gonna be the two of us for a couple of days until conditions improve. The captain said the seas are just too choppy to take the vessel out. The dive team is on standby and will be ready to go once this foul weather subsides. As you can well imagine, they are still very distraught over Calvin's tragic death. He was a well-respected and highly-esteemed member of the dive team."

"What the hell happened out there anyway," I asked.

"No one really knows for sure. We're still waiting for the results of the autopsy and toxicology report to come out. They say he got drunk and fell overboard in the middle of the night. They discovered him missing when he didn't show up for breakfast the following morning. The Coast Guard found his body washed up on the beach several days later."

"Dr. Stephens seems to think he may have committed suicide…?"

"I don't think so, Peter. I mean, I didn't really know Calvin very well, but he seemed like a rational person. He was a family man, you know. He was an excellent scuba diver and he had big dreams of piloting his own ship one day and retiring in the Greek Isles."

"Hmm...Did he have a history of sleepwalking or insomnia?"

"Not that I'm aware of, but I guess that's certainly a possibility." She paused for a moment. "Are you ready to go? I just need to stop at my place and pick up my things before we head down there. Here, let me help you with your bags, sir!"

When I first embarked on my journey half a world away on that beautiful spring day in May, I never imagined in my wildest dreams that I would actually encounter these cyclopean cephalopod creatures, let alone do battle with them. Looking back on it now, I realize there is no rational explanation for the bizarre and otherworldly sequence of events I endured that day. As to whether they were merely the figments of an overactive imagination, the drug-induced hallucinations of a heightened state of consciousness, or the hellish visions of a horribly vivid nightmare in which my mind had been altered, I cannot say.

We drove down the coastal highway through the pouring rain in her old beat up Land Rover and got into Maggona Beach before nightfall. We were welcomed graciously by the innkeepers and served a tasty seafood gumbo with tangy curry sauce and hot bread. After dinner the jet lag finally caught up with me and I had to excuse myself early. I conked out as soon as I hit the bed and slept like a log until morning.

Professor Khandir pulled over and parked the Land Rover on the side of the road and started unloading our gear. There was a warm tropical breeze coming off the ocean, but the heavy rain was relentless, the sweltering heat unbearable, and the oppressive humidity stifling, making things just plain miserable. "The estuary is just down on the other side of those mangroves. Once the tides recede, we'll be able to slosh around in the mud for as long as we want."

"I take it this isn't your first visit to Maggona Beach?"

"Are you kidding? I was born and raised on this part of the island." She smiled reminiscently and gazed out over the stormy sea. "You know, Peter, when I was younger, I was marveled by the wild tales I used to hear about a colossal sea creature roaming around out there in the depths. Turns out it was just an elaborate hoax concocted by the local fishermen to scare off the competition and keep them from dipping their nets in these waters."

We managed to fit all of our equipment into two backpacks, along with some rope in case one of us happened to get stuck in the mud. She pulled out a pair of four-foot-long bamboo sticks from the back of the Land Rover and handed me one. "These will help us poke our way through the muck and keep us from sinking in too far." Covered from head to toe in rain gear, we slowly made our way down the makeshift trail to Maggona Beach.

Nestled between the bay to the south and a tiny fishing village, whose name I can't even pronounce, to the north, Maggona Beach is nothing more than a narrow strip of shoreline roughly ten miles long and fifty to sixty yards wide where the mouth of the Maggona River empties into the Indian Ocean. On a clear day they say you can see the Maldives from the surrounding hills. But not today.

Even though high tide was not due for another four or five hours, the gale force winds were still powerful enough to produce some pretty hefty waves, kicking up sand in our faces. The patches of mangroves were interspersed with palm trees and some type of tall tropical swamp grass which caused me to sneeze and wheeze and made wading through the muck extremely challenging. We trudged tirelessly along the beach for a mile or two before finally reaching a network of estuaries and salt marshes. The beach was deserted except for a few blue-footed booby birds. I guess we were the only fools crazy enough to be out in these deplorable conditions. The swamps and mudflats were swollen with rainwater and there were several good-sized tide pools that had formed, which looked as though they'd be perfect habitat to search for Periophthalmus. The beach was teeming with all sorts of strange crustaceans, so it was no surprise when we came across a small colony of mudskippers burrowing in and out of the sand. I pulled out my trusty Minolta and started shooting close-ups of the silly little critters as they splashed about from puddle to puddle, foraging for crabs and other arthropods. "Well, there's certainly no shortage of blennies around here, eh professor…?" But she didn't respond. She seemed distracted and looked over my shoulder. Something else had caught her attention.

I turned to see what it was that had Aggie sidetracked. It was a small flock of seagulls and some pelicans circling overhead, and they were swooping down at something very large half-buried in the sand. "What on earth is that...?" I grabbed my binoculars and focused in on the dark object through the mist. At first, I thought it might have been a submarine or a downed aircraft. Then I realized what I was seeing. "Holy cow! I think it's a whale carcass. Here take a look."

I passed her the field glasses and she adjusted her sights. "My God! I think you're right. It is a whale, and an awful big one by the looks of it. We better go take a look. Maybe it's still breathing."

We tromped through the mud, the driving rain pelting our hoods, the howling winds buffeting our faces, slowing our pace down to a mere crawl. When we got to within five hundred feet of the carcass, the unmistakable stench of death hit us like a freight train, and we had to cover our noses with handkerchiefs. "Good God, that smells horrible." The stench was rancid, and we were forced to breathe through our mouths as we crept closer to the rotting mammoth. The foul stench was nauseating, and I started to gag. The flies were everywhere, and we had to shoo them away just to keep them from going down our throats.

The carcass lay on its side partially submerged in the surf, its stomach and intestines ripped open and disemboweled. We carefully circled around to the front for a closer look. It was the remains of a fifty-foot sperm whale, its eyes gouged out of their sockets, its face completely eaten away. Bones had been splintered and the front of its skull had been picked clean. We both took a step back and covered our mouths, but Professor Khandir couldn't hold it in any longer and vomited all over her waders.

Then we saw them, hundreds of them, gnawing at the carcass and scavenging on the chunks of raw flesh they had torn off. They were more terrifying than I ever could have imagined. In fact, they were by far the most repulsive, sickening things I have ever seen, and will no doubt haunt my dreams for the rest of my days. They were a dark greenish color with pink and orange pigmentation on their cantaloupe-shaped heads, and they smelled as vile and as wretched as the carcass itself.

There had to be a hundred or more of these cyclopean cephalopod creatures tangled together like spaghetti in one enormous aggregated mass of rolling eyeballs, twisted tentacles and sharp bloody fangs. Their arm-like tentacles were lined with tiny suction cups which they used to cling to the carcass and viciously devour the rotting flesh. The sands of Maggona Beach had been turned into one gigantic grotesque pool of blood, sea foam, slime, whale guts and blubber.

Suddenly a small cluster of these fishy invertebrates started creeping toward us, making a squishy, squashy sound as they skittered across the wet sand. We took another step back, their big protruding eyes watching our every move. And using their flexible tentacles like springboards to propel themselves a good ten or twelve feet in the air, they catapulted. We swatted them away with our bamboo sticks and most of the creatures scattered. But one of them landed at my feet, and in a fit of rage I stomped on it, flattening it like a pancake and proceeded to beat it to death with my flask. It flinched and made a horrible squealing noise as it flopped around in the muck before finally giving up the ghost.

More of them came at us from behind. One of the larger creatures lunged aggressively and latched onto the back of Professor Khandir's leg. She let out a blood-curdling scream as it tore through her clothes and punctured her skin. It dug hard into her flesh, penetrating deeper while she fought desperately to brush it off. "Good God, Peter...Get this damn thing off me!" It wrapped one of its sticky tentacles around her waist and tried dragging her into the surf. She struggled to keep her balance and almost fell into the muck. I rushed over and jabbed the creature repeatedly with the tip of my bamboo stick until I was finally able to pry it loose. The creature fell to the sand, flailed around in the mud for a moment then scuttled off and burrowed itself beneath the carcass.

I snatched Aggie's hand and pulled her out of striking distance. She was having a hard time staying on her feet and I had to half carry her out of harm's way. I ran with her as fast as I could up the slope and found a footpath leading to the highway. Now I say ran, however, if you've ever tried running through mud and sand wearing heavy waders while trying to support an extra hundred and twenty pounds, you know it's more like a slow crawl. Nevertheless, I managed to get us both up the hill to safety but had to leave poor Professor Khandir waiting by the side of the road while I went and retrieved the Land Rover. She was in excruciating pain and had already lost a lot of blood. I lifted her up and gently placed her in the passenger seat. She was going into shock and I was afraid she might black out. I screeched out of there as fast as I could go and sped off to get help.

Despite a fairly nasty bite mark on her femur and a slight infection, the doctor had Aggie all stitched up and out of the hospital in less than twenty-four hours. The following day we stood in the pouring rain alongside a small group of local villagers on the ridge by the old lighthouse overlooking Maggona Beach and watched as a crew of hazmat workers in protective suits and gas masks bulldozed what was left of the whale carcass back out to sea.

RED, WHITE AND BLACK

Mark Cassell

Judy only knew his first name: Charlie. And he was dead.

He wore the same white clothes as her. Itchy and loose. White sneakers, too. Or trainers, as they said here in England. Only his, toes down over the bed, were spattered with blood. So much red in contrast to the glaring walls. Red, white…and black. A tar-like substance clung to the bed linen and spotted his clothes, merging with the blood. Clumps of that dark filth streaked the wall as though it had grown from the plaster.

The medication, the drugs, whatever they'd given her, still clogged her brain, and even a cry for help seemed beyond her.

She stepped back and her ass smacked the door frame. A lump filled her throat. She swallowed and breathed. She'd become accustomed to the institute's fresh paint smell but now the coppery stink of blood overpowered it—and also something like wet foliage or soggy vegetables.

The sheets were twisted around his body, his face pressed into the pillow. That black stuff streaked his neck and cheek. Whatever it was, it looked like it had suffocated him. His hands were dead claws. His arms, hairy and bloodied. Welts and blood-bruises curled around his forearm.

Just like her own.

She brushed her knuckles down her arm, over those peculiar welts and grazes. Still sore, and still she couldn't recall how she'd gotten them. Similar to Charlie's yet showed no sign of any black infection. Was this going to happen to her?

Earlier at dinner, he'd invited her to his room saying he had something for her to read—which could mean any number of things. However, she saw a newspaper heaped beside the bed and had no doubt that was it. The front page pictured a man wearing sunglasses, his face turned to the headline: DEATH OF A HERO. Above that it said, John Lennon Shot Dead in New York.

She snatched it up and stared at the portrait photo of her favourite Beatle. He wore a blazer, a shirt, and a loose necktie, and he looked smooth in those sunglasses. Shot dead? Her hands curled into fists and the paper crumpled. She tore her gaze from the newspaper, back to Charlie. The dark filth also caked his hair.

At least she couldn't see his face.

Her cheeks were warming, her breath quickening. Again, her thoughts dragged.

The last time she'd seen him alive, he had a spoon of pudding in his mouth and waved at her across the canteen. Her head ached and she'd needed to lay down. Everyone had responded differently, and she guessed that was the nature of a clinical trial. The doctors told them they'd be monitored over the next several weeks. She looked at the black muck, the way it oozed from his wounds. Whatever this was, it was one hell of a side effect. Perhaps other candidates had also died. She had to find someone, tell someone. She twisted the newspaper in her hands and the welts on her forearm appeared to wriggle—her vision pulsing like it had during dinner.

She had to get a grip on herself.

Charlie was dead. Lennon, too. This was a sick world she lived in. Lennon murdered in NYC. Her home, her city. The ceiling seemed to press down, lowering until it almost touched her scalp, the main house above pressing her into the earth. The thought of being in Britain—in the Garden of England, no less—felt truly absurd at that moment.

The newspaper slipped from her hands and fell with a slap. She blinked, focused, and her sneakers squeaked as she lurched into the corridor.

She called: "Help! Anyone? Help!"

Her voice shot along the strip lights and bounced back. Then silence.

The floor tiles sucked her feet and she staggered onward. She passed another room and a peek revealed a kaleidoscope of red, white, and black. She wasn't surprised. Her ill-fitting clothes flapped as her pace quickened. More rooms, each no different from Charlie's. Her head throbbed with every footfall. Just how long until this caught up with her?

She shouted, "Hello?"

Again, silence.

"Hell—"

From somewhere a burst of static answered. The sound crackled and faded.

An empty corridor led to another stretch of open doors, everyone revealing more death. And that black infection. The trial had clearly gone wrong.

Around a corner, along another corridor, Judy reached an area she'd often thought of as a reception. Usually there'd be a nurse or an orderly busying around. She approached the glass-fronted office—a smear of pink and grey misted the cracked glass.

Inside, a computer terminal with bulky casing took up most of the desk. A telephone, receiver missing, sat dwarfed by a stack of manila files. The coiled wire draped across a lady's wrist. One blue fingernail pointed in accusation at a black smudge on the desk.

An earthy stink filled Judy's nostrils. She held her breath and took another step forward.

Slumped in a swivel chair was the nurse, Mary. Or May. Judy almost felt guilty in forgetting and refused to get close enough to read her name tag. Those familiar shades of gore covered the woman's uniform. Her neck stretched, head back, hair dangling to the tiles. Her white hat rested in a red pool. That black matter splayed across the tiles.

Perhaps this had nothing to do with the trials and was instead some kind of outbreak, some fatal disease.

A sound—rustling?—echoed from further down the corridor. Another survivor? Thank God.

Her vision warped and she stumbled, backing out of the office.

A rustling, shuffling sound, again and...

"Have you seen Kat?" A man's voice erupted from behind her and she spun and almost collapsed into his arms.

Parker.

His eyes, piercing, blue. His hair, ruffled. Sweat beaded his forehead. "Judy. Where is Kat?"

Often this doctor—she'd assumed he was one of the important doctors behind these trials—would bring his daughter in. A cute child, about four or five years old with flaming hair and inquisitive eyes. Judy focused on the room beyond him. Colouring books scattered the floor and crayons were crushed into the tiles like rainbow splinters.

"Have you seen her?" He grabbed Judy's shoulders. Along his forearm, running parallel with his veins were familiar black marks. No red welts though. He released her and stepped back. He shouted, "Kat!"

Shaking her head sent silver spots darting across her vision. She straightened her back. "What's happened here?"

"We have to find Kat."

"Yes. I'll help. Why is everyone—"

"Dead?"

She nodded. More silver spots.

"We must find Kat." He charged towards the double doors. With palms flat, he shoved them wide and disappeared into the next room.

Judy followed. It was kind of like a classroom, where she and perhaps a dozen others sat when first introduced to the trial ahead. She'd sat at the back next to Charlie—dead!—whom at the time she'd not known. They were all there for the same reason: money. Judy recognised an eagerness in everyone's eyes and wondered if she looked the same. Clinical trials offered a lot of money these days. Apparently, it had something to do with the patients already here at the institute but although Parker gave them a tour, they weren't allowed to see any patients. Prohibited access, he'd said and added that they were expanding departments.

Across the room, Parker yanked open a door to a stationery cupboard. Swinging wide, the handle thumped the wall. He hardly resembled the confident doctor who'd once stood before them, smiling and concluding that most of the underground sprawl here was an immense building project.

Judy felt useless, her mind reeling. This was all like a bad trip, feeling just as she had last year. Unlike some of her friends who spiralled into the madness of drug abuse, she'd been lucky to escape her teens. This had been the beginning of a new life for her. At least, that was the intention.

Parker barged past her and out of the room. "Help me."

She pressed her palms to her temples and followed. "Sorry."

In the corridor, his mouth turned down at the corners, he shouted, "Kat!"

Music crackled from somewhere like a radio had been switched on. It came in faint waves. Judy couldn't make out the tune.

Parker frowned and headed for an archway, into another corridor. "Kat?"

His pounding footfalls echoed, and Judy staggered after him. Her stomach somersaulted but at least her vision was sharpening. Into the corridor, those strip lights a harsh glare, she squinted. Parker had vanished. Three doors lined a wall. The paint smell filled her nostrils and somehow cleansed her mind. Only a fraction.

A door creaked. She rushed for it and pushed it open. Her vision blurred. The wood was cold—even that seemed to clear her head a little more.

Crouched between filing cabinets, hugging his red-haired daughter, was Parker. He said her name over and over. Her arms wrapped around his neck and in a tiny fist a crayon poked between her fingers. A black one.

In a muffled voice, she said, "Daddy, where is everybody?"

He didn't reply, only squeezed her.

High in the corner of the room more of the black filth peppered the walls and ceiling, resembling damp spores. The house above was old so she guessed the foundations would be just as old. Surely where they were expanding the underground part of the institute, damp spores wouldn't set in so soon. In truth, she had no idea.

Parker stood, lifting Kat into his arms. His smile said everything.

Kat's eyes were wide and round. She still clutched the crayon. "Hello," she said to Judy.

"Hi." Judy held the door open for them.

"Right," Parker said, his voice stronger than before. "Let's get out."

Her brain still felt sluggish. "What's going on?"

"I have no idea."

"But—"

He led them back to the office and made sure to face Kat away from the dead nurse. This time, Judy was close enough to read the name tag: Mary. The black stuff coated most of it and appeared to have melted the plastic.

Snatching the telephone, Parker prodded the buttons. After a moment's pause, he said, "Dead."

Judy again glanced at Mary.

Parker scratched his forearm. "We must assume it's taken everyone else."

"Why not us?"

He pulled Kat into his arms. His eyes seemed to shrink, and he looked down. "Come on."

They ran through a set of double doors, passing through several empty rooms. Beneath an archway, they entered a room unfamiliar to Judy. She assumed this was one of the prohibited areas.

Hypodermic needles lay scattered on the floor. Again, black marks streaked the tiles. Further back, the strip lights bathed a row of gurneys, the linen seemed to glow. One was occupied by a man, naked from the waist up and secured by wide leather straps. That black matter caked half his torso. His eyes bulged and blood covered his shaven head and smeared his cheek. His lip flopped between clenched teeth from where he'd bitten it off. Black filth glistened, protruding through torn flesh and broken bone like the stuff had risen from his throat and busted through his jaw. Even now, it dribbled from between bone splinters and bubbled onto the mattress. A tooth bounced and tittered across the tiles leaving bloody splashes.

What the hell was all this? Why had the three of them been spared? Parker had those marks on his arms, and her own red welts didn't look good. This was some kind of nasty infection, certainly. It was simply a matter of time. She hoped Kat would somehow be immune.

The doors on the other side of the room swung closed with a double slap. Alone. Judy's heart twisted and she threw herself at them. She entered a wide room and an overpowering smell of paint washed over her. Although familiar throughout the institute, in here it poured down her throat.

Kat stood beside her father, watching him pick up a crowbar.

Overturned paint tins littered the floor, their contents puddled from wall to wall. White, glistening, and fresh. A stepladder lay on its side, and footprints headed off beneath an archway and around a corner.

Parker lifted Kat with his free arm as Judy reached his side. Creating footprints of their own, they followed the other set to the corner.

And stopped.

Judy's breath snatched and she coughed.

"Don't look," Parker said to his daughter.

The body of a decorator huddled against the wall; his legs trapped by a mound of grey-black filth, his neck a ragged mess. Bloody handprints smeared the wall. Above, more filth—fungus—drooped from a hole. Finding a larger amount of that black matter, Judy now saw that it was indeed a type of fungus. Exposed wires coiled through its sweaty skin. They sparked.

That music again; a distant sound, crackling.

The strip lights buzzed, then surged and went out.

Kat screamed.

The yellow glow of emergency lights flooded the corridor.

The fungal growth above seethed, the shadows deepened, and the black mass rushed downward. Tendrils burst from its surface, flexing dozens of skinny fingers. One extended and with a wet slap, coiled around the decorator's leg to yank the body towards the ever-widening darkness. It was as though the shadows had opened up like a gaping mouth. The light dimmed further as the fungus clawed across the ceiling, the walls, the floor.

Parker held Kat away from the expanding darkness. A slithering tentacle whipped out, lashing for him. He swung the crowbar and the thing recoiled like a snake.

He shoved Kat into Judy's arms. "Take her!"

Judy hugged the child to her breast. More darkness splayed across the tiles, blending with the paint, the blood. Reaching out. This fungus had a life of its own. Impossible.

Again, Parker swung the crowbar and his leg shot sideways. He crashed to the floor and scrambled to his knees, slid, and smacked the wall. The tendrils drew back, ready to strike a second time.

"Come on!" Judy shouted and with one arm, yanked him upright.

Deep furrows creased his forehead. "Run!"

Judy fled down the corridor and in seconds reached an intersection.

From close behind, Parker yelled, "Go left!"

* * *

More fungus coated the walls and encased the occasional strip light. Sprinting beneath it, heading along that stretch, the darker the corridors became. Judy waited for the darkness to thrash at her. How was this happening? What they'd witnessed back there had been impossible.

After what seemed like a hundred corridors, they reached the elevators. The strip lights were all dead and the emergency lights pushed through deep shadows.

"What—" Parker began to say, and he staggered to a halt. One hand pressed against a wall, his chest heaving.

Kat's tears soaked into Judy's shirt. Her lungs burned and when she stepped closer to the elevators her stomach lurched. The fungus had stitched the doors together. Black fibers entwined like stubborn roots.

"Bloody hell!" Parker's knuckles whitened as he twisted the crowbar.

"The stairs?" she demanded. Kat was starting to feel heavy.

"There aren't any." His eyes narrowed.

"What?"

"We're far below ground. Only the lifts."

Lifts. She loved the British.

"There's another lift…on the other side." He pushed past her. "But I don't fancy the walk."

He raised the crowbar.

For a moment he paused, and again Judy heard the faint crackle of music from somewhere. As before, she couldn't quite make out the tune.

"Parker…" She breathed out, not realising she'd held her breath. It was as though she waited for that black stuff to come alive and grab him. She stepped further back.

He stabbed the crowbar between the elevator doors, leaned against it, and heaved. They didn't budge, nor made any difference to that fungal growth. He heaved again.

And the doors burst open.

A dark expanse of simply nothing lay beyond. A kind of liquid darkness shimmered like a diesel spill defying gravity. Parker tumbled headfirst into the yawning void. This time the blackness didn't look like fungus, it looked like the shadows themselves had opened up.

The doors slammed closed. Black threads crept inward and with a sound like dry leaves, stitched the doors together.

"Parker!" Judy backed up, turning Kat's head away and hugged her tighter. The weight of the girl brought the darkness closer. No stairs.

Judy turned and ran, heading back towards the intersection. She had to find the other elevator, wherever the hell it was. The fungus already crawled over the tiles, along the walls. Sure, there were scuffs from the gurneys, but the new flooring, the bright white walls, the brilliant glow of those strip lights, all highlighted the creeping spores.

She shoulder-barged a set of double doors and lurched into another room. Her heartbeat seemed to echo in the emptiness. From an archway at the far end, music drifted towards her. Recognition. It was a Beatles tune: Hey Jude... John Lennon was dead. Shot dead—she still couldn't believe it. So many thoughts crashed through her brain. Her arms ached and her legs felt like jello. She slowed her pace and stopped before the archway. On the other side, another corridor; bright, white, and no darkness. There didn't appear to be any spore patches, either.

She placed Kat down.

Hey Jude...

The girl looked up at her and then around the room. Wide eyed, red face, puffy. Her cheeks glistened. "Where's daddy?"

Judy swallowed, her mouth and lips dry. "He's... He'll be with us soon." She hated herself for saying that.

The music seemed not too far away. Jude, Judy... Her father used to call her that, before alcohol made him call her other things, before alcohol forced his hand against her mother. She recalled how once she'd had to clean up blood from the kitchen floor. That slap and swish creating pink arcs, the radio playing in the background as she wiped away Mother's agony. Slap, swish.

Judy lifted Kat and headed off, praying she'd find the elevator soon. As she rounded a corner...

Slap, swish.

Diluted blood smeared in an arc. And that sound: slap, swish. Beside a bucket over-spilling with pink froth was the janitor, mop in hand. His blue uniform flapped around him. Blood splashed his shoes.

The strip light overhead flickered, and in a burst of static the music faded.

Slap, swish.

Judy's pace slowed. Finally, someone else was here, someone else to help.

Kat's tiny arms looped Judy's neck, and in a muffled voice she said, "I want to walk."

"No," Judy whispered. They were only a few paces away from the janitor. She hoped he wasn't contagious and moved closer to the wall. "Help us," she said to him.

Still he kept his head down. His voice croaked as he said, "I must clean this up."

"Help us!"

"It's that damned harvest."

"What?"

The blood left little room for them to pass.

"Such a mess," he said and raised his head. White teeth shone through a bushy beard, his hair just as unkempt. "Stevenson and his damned harvest."

She had no time for this. "Which way—"

"Stevenson. The boss. Not the boss-boss, but the boss down here." Sweat dotted his brow.

"What are you talking about?" she snapped.

He pushed his hand against the wall. Spores bloomed from the surface, approaching his fingers. His flesh darkened and a greyness crept under his sleeve, up his neck and into his face. His mouth went slack and his eyes moistened, then blackened. They shone like black marbles. No white, just solid black orbs bulging in hollow sockets. Between pale lips, his teeth flashed again.

She pressed against the opposite wall, praying that the spores wouldn't reach for her.

He removed his hand from the wall and gripped the mop. Slap, swish.

She squeezed past.

"Such a mess." He continued to mop the floor, but only succeeded in slopping the blood around. His efforts hastened. Pink water splashed the walls, consumed by the spores.

Slap, swish… Swish, swish.

The sound of the man's frantic cleaning faded behind her and the music crackled into play again.

Hey Jude.

By now, Judy's throat pulsed with its own heartbeat. Her arms were killing her—putting Kat down seemed like a good idea but she couldn't. She had to find the other elevator.

The music increased in volume, the notes sharper, the vocals more defined.

Mind reeling, she reluctantly placed Kat down. The girl's feet tiptoed and then she stood on her own. The square tiles warped and shrank. They seemed miles away and vertigo tugged at Judy's legs, her stomach. Kat peered up from far away, her eyes wide, just as Judy closed her own into a welcome darkness, albeit brief, private. Paul McCartney's vocals floated towards her in waves. She straightened, eyes remaining closed. This was crazy. And someone was playing with her, playing that Beatles tune over and over.

"What's your name?" Kat's voice leaked through the darkness, nudging aside Paul's chorus.

Inhaling the smell of paint, she opened her eyes. Kat's hair, waves of orange and red, burned through the threatening darkness.

"I'm called Kat," she said.

"I know." Judy's voice sounded weird. "I'm Judy."

The little girl nodded. "Where are we going?"

"Getting out of here." She stroked Kat's cheek—clammy—and then lifted her up. The girl somehow weighed more than she had earlier.

Still that tune crackled from invisible speakers.

* * *

Kat fidgeted in Judy's arms as she jogged through more rooms. All empty save for the odd gurney or two, all showed signs of that black stuff coating the wall. The music swept along with them, sometimes soft, sometimes loud. Always crackling, as though played from scratched vinyl. Perhaps it was from a record player. High in the corners, she saw several brackets and wire coiling from holes. No speakers.

The smell of damp, of foliage, eventually overtook the paint smell, and the strip lights seemed to be either off or not working. Only the emergency lights guided them. It appeared this was where they were still building the place. Some walls were just plasterboard panels and the ground was simply bare concrete. A wheelbarrow contained three paint tins and a bucket of paintbrushes.

Perhaps given time, they'd build that staircase. She guessed—she hoped—the elevator would be somewhere near.

Then the lights went out. Deep, dark, suffocating.

Not even any emergency lights.

Kat screamed. It echoed, shrill. Her fingers dug into Judy's neck.

"It's okay," she told the girl, stroking her hair. She didn't know if she reassured Kat or herself.

The music had stopped, and so had they.

Something creaked—a door?—from beside them. A vertical strip of light speared the darkness, a pathetic illumination.

Kat made a mewling sound like an animal.

The door swung wide and smacked the wall. The echo died as the music resumed, this time from within the room and no longer crackling. A miasma of damp, decay, and that heavy stink of vegetation forced itself down into her lungs.

Beyond the doorway, a vortex of yellows and browns churned and filled the room from floor to ceiling, wall to wall. Sweat prickled Judy's forehead as she struggled to comprehend what she faced. Kat clamped to her neck. Even though Judy thought of how the elevator doors had jerked open and swallowed Parker, she couldn't move. She had to but couldn't. Whatever this was it curdled like mud and oil, milk and gravy. It hurt to look at yet was mesmerizing.

Still the music washed over her.

Judy squinted, knowing she must run. Amid the roiling chaos, the colours merged and twisted like teasing shadows, like phantoms in a sickly mist. Contours formed, sharpened; outlines of something…of furniture? Yes, a table and chairs, walls and picture frames. The haze thinned out, the browns becoming yellows and spiralling into cleaner colours, pleasant, soothing, normal. Sharp, three-dimensional and familiar.

Way too familiar.

Hey Jude…

She licked her lips. This was a dining room, her dining room—or at least, her parents' dining room.

A remaining coil of shadow swooped down and around the turntable of the stereo system. Darkness spinning, coiling with the rotating vinyl. Faint wisps joined it and vanished into the stylus.

Her heart felt like a brick. What was this? And the music filled her up, stormed her ears.

The doorframe seemed to buckle, swept up into the surrounding shadows, torn apart silently. She stood in the centre of the dining room. The tune rose in volume, rumbling from the twin speakers either side of the record player. From the direction of the kitchen she heard Mother preparing dinner.

Judy realised she was holding her breath and mouthed, No.

Kat released her leg. "Where are we?"

Judy blinked. When had she set Kat down? She didn't recall letting her go. She stepped forward. "Kat…"

The girl stood beside the oak table, its scuffed surface still marked by the red paint Judy had spilled—oh, how father had struck her hard.

She threw glances around the room.

Kat walked further forward and looked around. She passed straight through a chair as though it wasn't there. Of course, it wasn't there, none of this was real. Everything was a cruel phantom, a tease from Judy's past, a taunt of a childhood she so desperately wanted to leave in New York. This all had to be due to the clinical trial. Some bad trip, a hallucination triggered perhaps by the chemicals she'd abused in her teens and now the ones the doctors had given her.

She lifted her arm and looked at the welts and blood-bruises. What happened to her?

The little girl continued to walk and passed through the table. Her hair seemed to glow in contrast to the illusion. Through the table, passing the red stain that was now fading wisps of shadow rose like smoke. Kat turned and lowered herself to sit on something Judy couldn't see. Whatever it was, it made her bounce. Perhaps it was a cushion under the table—but this was all an illusion. The now-shimmering mirage of the table almost obscured the girl.

Judy moved, her eyes darting to the left and right, over to the fading archway. The clatter of cutlery, of dishes, reverberated from beyond. Her mother was there.

Her tongue stuck to the roof of her mouth.

Hey Jude...

Kat looked up as a shadow emerged from the kitchen. Someone approached. It wasn't Judy's mother, couldn't be. Her mother was dead, killed by her father. Could it be her father? No, impossible, his suicide had closely followed.

Judy felt as small as Kat. The drugs they'd fed her were really playing with her, dragging up unwanted memories.

The bulk of shadow filled the archway and finally someone emerged. She couldn't see the face. A white smock, stained dark, somehow pushed aside the wispy shadows, the image, the illusion. Lights flickered around the figure—candles, there were candles. No longer lampshades, and not even strip lights. Just candles.

Her phantom past, the music, all shrank and dropped back to where it belonged: the past. None of this should be here. The room faded, and in its place the rocky expanse of a cavern stretched out, its gloom lit only by the candles. Moisture dampened the air; ammonia stung her nostrils. Where was she? As the final wisps of shadow lifted, the false room completely vanished. This appeared to be the end of the labyrinth of rooms and corridors beneath the institute. Rock and masonry heaped the floor, and a number of concrete pillars reached into the darkness overhead. A stretch of unpainted wall lined one end of this great chamber. The blank-faced plaster looked out of place, foreign next to the curved, dark hulks of rock. The candles flickered, their haloes offering little comfort.

"Hello." The man's voice pierced the gloom. Deep, commanding. She recognised it. It belonged to Stevenson, the boss, the man in charge of the trials. This was the second time she'd met Stevenson. The first was when she'd sat in the room with the other candidates, when she'd signed the consent forms thinking only of the money.

Judy raked her fingers through her hair. Her head ached.

"Did the darkness make you see something?" he asked.

Judy glared at him. She didn't know what to say. None of this made sense. Earlier the janitor had said something about Stevenson's harvest. What had he meant?

"Hello, Kat." He smiled and slid his hands into his pockets.

Kat said, "Hi." Her back was twisted as she peered behind her and stared up at the man. She sat on a stained mattress. Leather straps, like serpents, coiled next to her. The buckles glinted with a dull wink from the candles lining an outcrop of rock. The archway behind Stevenson—no longer the archway to the phantom kitchen—framed him. It made his presence even larger, made him loom over Kat. Over them both.

The man approached. His moustache twitched.

"You're Judy," he said.

She nodded. "What's going on? What have you done to us? Everyone else is dead. Are my hallucinations anything to do with you? The trial?"

"What did you see?"

"We have to get out of here!"

Something clanked.

Kat had reached behind her and now dragged something over the mattress. "What's this?" She pulled an hourglass into view. Scuffed wood, scratched bulbs; the thing looked ancient. What appeared to be a wrist harness swung from it. Its buckles clanked again.

Stevenson's grin pushed his mouth wide, thick lips glistening. "That, young lady, is the hourglass." He put emphasis on the word hour.

Kat clutched it and looked into the lower bulb. She shook it. "It's old. What's it for?"

"Put it down," Judy yelled. Whatever it was, it was unnatural. And Stevenson had a hand in all this. "Don't touch it!"

Kat shuddered. Her bottom lip quivered.

"No need to be like that." Stevenson stepped around the mattress and stood beside a computer terminal that squatted on the floor. Wires and cables poked from it. The blank screen reflected the hourglass and Kat's tiny hands. "It's a method of extracting darkness."

"What?" Judy's voice sounded tiny even to herself.

The little girl's chin trembled, tears welling.

"The clinical trial is only half of it. This…" He waved his hand over Kat's head. "…Is what really matters."

Judy crouched beside the mattress. She took the girl's hand and whispered, "I'm sorry."

Kat said nothing, staring into her lap. The hourglass rested against her thigh.

"There's a darkness within us," Stevenson said. "Within us all."

"We have to go." Judy grabbed Kat's arm. "Come on."

Stevenson's voice drifted over her shoulder. "That magnificent device allows us to tap it."

Pain. Sharp at the base of her skull. An explosion of colour…

Then nothing.

* * *

Tangled images threaded together, and Judy struggled to make sense of them: shadowy tentacles snatching Kat's father into the elevator; the janitor mopping blood; black spores spreading across the walls…and the turntable, spinning round and round and round. Hey Jude. The black void swallowing her.

Judy's consciousness sharpened, and now the sound of creaking leather, of clanking buckles, drifted through the dark. Her eyelids cracked open. Wide.

The air snatched in her throat.

She lay on her side, the cold ground biting through her clothes. Her ankles were bound to her wrists, her back hunched. Rope dug into her already-enflamed flesh. She recognised the rock walls and the archway a short distance from her. And the mattress.

Kat was on it. The girl's eyes were closed, her breathing rhythmic as though she slept—unconscious but alive. Her legs and arms were spread, wrists and ankles fastened by leather straps. One tiny hand curled around the lower bulb of the hourglass, secured by the attached harness. The computer hummed and a series of commands ran down the green screen. Bunched wires coiled from the main unit and connected to electrode pads that stuck to the girl's temples.

Judy's heart lurched. "Leave her alone!"

Stevenson stepped into view. "You're just in time."

"What are you doing to her?" she demanded and tried to kick out, only to succeed in sliding sideways. Her back hit the rock wall. "She's just a girl!"

"Yes, that's why I'm seeing what her darkness will be. Your coming here is a stroke of luck, wouldn't you say?"

"Let us go!"

"The hourglass will connect with her darkness," he said. "It's a 17th-century device once used to extract the evil from supposed witches."

"What?" Judy struggled to sit up. Failed.

"A remarkable apparatus," he added.

She glanced at her wrists, the rope binding them, and those welts, the pinches. Her stomach knotted, and she knew that she'd once been attached to this hourglass. "You're...you're behind the infection."

"It could be a type of infection, certainly." He shrugged and glanced at Kat. "But it's more than that."

Judy wriggled. Her back ached and her head thumped. It felt sticky from where Stevenson had evidently knocked her out. "This is madness."

"Darkness is the root of our madness."

A wave of nausea rushed in on her. She gulped, refusing to spew. Her breath came in gasps. She had to save Kat.

"That's right, calm down."

From an angle, Judy saw chalk markings on the rock face beside her. Words? Symbols? She didn't recognise any. One, however, could've been a crude diagram of the hourglass itself. Silvery spots peppered her vision. Those markings blurred for a moment; they looked like real voodoo crap, some kind of occult bullshit that belonged in those absurd Hammer horror films these Brits seemed to love. Gritting her teeth, her ears ringing, she focused on Kat, and on the hourglass. The white sand in the lower bulb looked innocent enough. Perhaps extracting the darkness would somehow cleanse her, or would it infect her? But she was only a child. And what did this darkness have to do with madness? Again, Judy struggled against her bonds.

"Why are you doing this?" she shouted and kicked.

"We need to wait a while longer, then we can begin." He watched the computer monitor. "Not long."

More commands scrolled down the screen.

Judy thought of what the Janitor had said. "Something to do with your harvest?"

Stevenson's eyes narrowed. "You shouldn't know about that."

"Is it?"

"Most likely, yes." He again glanced at the computer. "Okay, we have time."

He crouched beside her. From a pocket he pulled out a Swiss Army knife, then cut her ankle bindings.

"Come with me." He grabbed her still-bound wrists and yanked her up.

She grunted, pain burning the back of her head. With a final look at Kat—so peaceful—Judy swayed.

Stevenson tugged her beneath the archway. Still gripping her arm, he threw open a door with his other hand. "I'm proud of this."

She squinted as a dozen or more spotlights burned into the gloom. The stink of vegetation, of rot, of mould, reached down Judy's throat.

"That idiot Parker never even knew," Stevenson whispered.

Judy's stomach twisted. "Oh my God."

Beneath metal framework, four gurneys lined a wall. Naked bodies occupied them. Male or female, she had no idea. Every mattress was stained brown and dotted with dark spores. Clamping apparatus held open the chest cavities where fungus growths bulged. Like gigantic black slugs, throbbing—with a heartbeat?—they seethed and converged overhead amongst the frame. The skin glistened and reflected the spotlights. Most of the ceiling had vanished in an expanse of sweating grey-black flesh, pulled taut like a grotesque canopy. Spores peppered the floor and the spotlight bases, the walls and the remainder of the ceiling.

Stevenson smiled.

Something—someone—groaned.

"Dear God, no," whispered Judy.

One of the bodies twitched and the head moved. A man. His eyes wandered as though drunk and his agony hissed through clenched teeth. Fungal tentacles swung from his chin.

Beneath his gurney, a darkness clustered in wispy shadows. A coiling pseudopod heaved and slits along its length puffed more spores, more shadows, to cloud the air. It hurt to look at; the way it kind of played with reality. Even as she watched, another tendril of shadow reached up to clutch the ceiling. It shifted aside the tiles. One fell and smacked the floor, cracking in two.

More pseudopods whipped the air, again the slits opening like mouths and belching clouds of shadow.

"Beautiful, isn't it?" Stevenson left her in the doorway and strolled into the centre of the room. He held his hands wide. "I have discovered the darkness inside us all."

Tendrils slithered towards him and stroked his shoes. This fungus had a life of its own, so did it know this man was its creator? Did he control the fungus, the shadows? Chasing his own desire to find the darkness at mankind's core—the very heart of madness—he'd clearly gone mad himself. Perhaps he'd inhaled the spores or even the shadows that now puffed from more slits along the tentacles. Did he once attach himself to the hourglass?

Judy gaped as the sentient clusters of darkness caressed his legs.

Those dark clouds were similar to the shadows that earlier had coiled from the phantom record player. She'd been attached to that hourglass at some point during her stay here, of that she had no doubt. That's why the shadows had revealed her past, it was her own darkness tangled with unwanted memories; a madness waiting for her.

She had to stop this. She had to rescue Kat before the computer loaded and the hourglass began whatever it was going to do to her.

Judy held her breath, hunched, and darted forward. Her shoulder smashed into Stevenson's stomach and he stumbled backwards. Driven by momentum, she almost went with him as he crashed into a gurney. The overhead frames screeched across the floor, and the fleshy sacks ruptured. Great plumes of shadow and spores fluttered. And embraced him.

He didn't have time to scream.

Only his feet and one arm stuck from the quivering mass as it ballooned. The other gurneys shifted, and the clamping mechanisms snapped closed. Shreds of black flesh flapped about and muffled the crunch of breaking ribs. Brackets and rods sprung sideways, clattering off the tiles. Some hit the fungus sacks with a thump. The main mass, once supported by the frame, had drooped. Metal groaned, shrieked, then snapped. The bulbous thing collapsed and slapped the ground.

Slime splashed Judy's face as she rolled away.

A seething yellow goo spread across the tiles. Pseudopods whipped and jerked, lashed and clawed at the tiles.

She scrambled to her feet.

More clamps pinged and clattered across the room. One of the bodies fell with a wet thump. A splay of black matter leaked from the gaping stomach. The dark clouds, the shadows, reached out—almost as if in comfort.

Stevenson's legs vanished.

Judy, cursing her bound wrists, staggered. She slipped, almost went down again, and lurched for the door.

Making it around the corner and beneath the archway, she dropped to her knees beside Kat. A glance at the computer and it appeared as though the column of data was slowing. She tugged the wires and the electrodes popped from the child's head. The screen went blank.

From behind her something else clattered, the light from the doorway shrinking. Without looking, she knew the pulsating mass of whatever-the-hell-it-was filled the doorway. Or perhaps it was the shadows. She fumbled the straps that fastened Kat's ankles, releasing them. Then those at her wrists. No time to remove the hourglass harness. The device thumped Judy's leg as she scooped up the girl and hoisted her over a shoulder—awkward with bound wrists. The rope pinched.

She backed out from the chamber, into the dark corridor, and jogged beneath the welcoming glow of emergency lights that looped from bare plasterboard panels. The elevator had to be here, or maybe another exit somewhere.

The area widened into an unfinished mess. The plasterboard gave way to rock either side. Further ahead where girders lined the ceiling and pushed into rock, a chain-link fence stretched out and separated them from a construction area.

Kat flopped in her arms and the hourglass smacked her thigh. Judy began to limp, heading for what she assumed was a chained gate in the fence. Perhaps they'd be able to squeeze through. Beyond this, deep in shadow—natural, she hoped—were what looked like pallets piled with bricks. Yes. There were bags of cement, too. There was even a forklift truck. There had to be an exit that way.

Her legs were killing her, and her arms screamed from awkwardly holding Kat.

She knew the darkness spread behind—her skin itched like a million ants crawled over her. The closer she got to the fence, the more she saw a faint light far on the other side of the construction area. Yes, she'd made it. No elevator, but sunlight? Two horizontal stretches of light cut through the gloom. From a pair of huge metal doors.

"What's happening?" Kat's muffled voice sounded sleepy. "It hurts."

"Nearly there." Judy coughed. Thank God Kat was okay.

"Hurts!" the girl whined. Blood covered her hand and dripped from the harness, the hourglass swinging.

And Judy tripped.

Her kneecaps smacked the ground, an elbow too. The girl tumbled from her grasp and sprawled, crying. Her eyes glinted in the brightening light, face screwed up.

A familiar crushing dizziness washed over Judy. She pressed the ground with her bound wrists and tried to get up.

"Run!" she shouted.

Kat stared past Judy's head. Her eyes widened and she screamed.

Judy pushed herself up, head swimming, and scrambled to her feet. She grabbed the girl, yanked her upright.

"Run!"

Staggering, the two of them crashed into the fence. Not quite a gate. It rattled. Judy's fingers curled around the chain. Cold. No way through. Her heart punched her throat. Her knees throbbed. She tugged the padlock. Locked. Closer to the ground there was a gap, big enough for Kat to squeeze through.

"There!" she yelled. "Under there!"

Kat obeyed and pushed her body beneath the fence. The hourglass went with her.

A glance over Judy's shoulder revealed the darkness clawing the rock walls. She looked back at Kat, who in turn stared up at her through the mesh. Her hair clumped across a grimy forehead. Red circles marked her temples from where Stevenson had attached the electrode pads.

"Run!" Judy poked her finger through the links in the fence, pointing at the sunlight. "That way."

With a quivering jaw, Kat turned and ran. The hourglass scraped along the ground like a medieval toy. Her footsteps echoed.

There was nothing at hand to break the padlock. Still the darkness spread across the rocks, flowing and tracing the contours, reaching for her. A combination of liquid shadow and black seething fungus crawling at her, plunging her into a deeper gloom.

She shook the fence and dropped to the ground. She pressed herself against the gap, shuffling sideways, willing herself to shrink. She clawed the ground.

Two fingernails broke. Pain exploded up her hand.

Around her, the light dimmed. The darkness closed in.

Far away, Kat shoved open the huge door. A metallic shriek rang out. The setting sun flared around the little girl's silhouette and for a moment she swam in blinding orange, the hourglass trailing behind.

Judy stopped trying to push through the gap. Kat was safe, that was all that mattered.

As sunlight swallowed Kat, the darkness swallowed Judy.

Six Seconds of Courage

Blaze Ward

The door slammed and they were safe.

For the moment.

At least Miguelito hoped so.

Him as the only Human, three Eland, and the last surviving member of the team, a Grace woman named Teela. That was it. And they nearly hadn't made it this far.

Teela reprogrammed the hatch to stay locked, regardless of the monsters on the other side trying to open it.

Miguelito studied the other three as she worked. He was used to seeing people with their faces painted in the traditional sugar skull to mark the Dia de la Muerte, but it still weirded him out to see it on an alien face. Even the Eland, for whom it was now a cultural thing.

They called themselves The Lost. A species that had fled their dying home-world on giant sleeper ships, NAFAL across the stars looking for a new home. One of those ships had found the Kekik network, named after the species, that had built it. The same ones that had found Humans originally.

Less than a decade after joining Kekik space, the Lapsyne invasion had nearly wiped out everyone and everything. The Eland had fled immediately, staying ahead of the invaders just like Miguelito's ancestors, that Hispanic underclass that had been relegated by the Anglos and Asians to being servants for the most part.

Miguelito had never been all that religious growing up, but he appreciated the Eland around him now. Noted how serious they took things, wearing the sugar skulls even in the middle of a derelict exploration.

There was no flexibility in the calendar, after all.

That helped calm him enough that his heart rate stopped racing so hard. Tradition.

The team boss was an older Eland, of the type called an astronomer because they were the ones always seeking the other stars where the rest of their kind might be found. Hopefully, the other Eland were safe from the Lapsyne because there were no jump-gates currently connecting connected to those systems. This one called himself Strider Blue, but that was just the public name. All the Eland had personal names that only got shared with the closest friends and family.

And while the rest of this team had known each other for decades, Miguelito was still the outsider here. They might consider each other family, but the woman warrior with a spear, the one known as Iron Scarab, just called him "Human," not even bothering with his name.

"Have we lost them?" Strider asked, breathless after that long run that had gotten the team through one of the giant cargo bays that had been strewn with abandoned cargo boxes.

Miguelito had kept up. The alternative was being killed and eaten by one of the Lapsyne monsters back there somewhere.

Two of the four Eland warriors had survived that first crazy ambush: Iron Scarab and Ellis Glenraven.

She was the tallest Eland Miguelito had even met, as she drew herself up to that amazing height and sneered angrily backwards at the hatch, her pale sugar skull making the woman look like a demon. Horns spiraling out of her forehead and up to lethal points just contributed to the image.

She shook her weird spear once, as if warding off evil.

"We have not lost them," she growled. "I warned that fool not to open that hatch before Teela checked the space beyond, but when has he ever listened to a woman?"

Miguelito turned to the gunman Eland standing next to him.

"Let me look at that," he ordered, tapping the man on the unwounded shoulder.

Ellis Glanraven had taken his public name from Human literature, so he tended to stand out with Eland as well as Humans. He was small as their kind went. Not exactly tiny, since he was still taller than most Humans, but more compact than most Eland. Like Iron Scarab, his face was painted, but Ellis had gone for far more colors, like jewels implanted in his fur.

Ellis put his bolter away in the holster and slipped off his jacket.

"It's not that bad," the gunman said defensively, but he turned his side so that Miguelito could inspect the wound.

Short slash just above the shoulder blades, but it had been mostly deflected by the armor in the jacket.

"You're still lucky the Three-Dub were expecting someone shorter," Miguelito teased. He and Ellis had known each other for many years in passing, so he could do that with this killer. The others were still strangers for the most part. "A Human might have gotten his head sliced off."

Three-Dub. The slang term for Wall-Walking-Warriors. Three dimensional fighters who could move like cats, jumping up and down without hurting themselves as they dropped from above or exploded out of holes to get you.

All the of the Lapsyne species were based on a hexapodal shape, just like the Kekik, those bipeds known as the Blues who had accidentally created these monsters.

As with the Blues, two legs and four arms were normal, although Lapsyne queens and nannies were Masters of Biology and had adapted their various warrior children forms as needed. Three-Dubs had slashing hands for the top pair, gripping hands for the second pair, and legs that let them jump like caffeinated anime squirrels.

Three of them had landed right in the middle of the group almost as soon as Strider's team was aboard the derelict, immediately killing the other two gunman, two Eland gunmen known as He Who Hunts and Bullseye, at the same time that one had slashed Ellis.

Right before Iron Scarab put her spear through the first creature and pinned him to the deck long enough for Miguelito to shoot the thing in the face. Then everyone had started shooting.

It had been twenty seconds of insane ferocity.

Miguelito didn't do violence. He was a medic. Still, he carried a pistol and explored derelicts trying to get rich, so it was an occupational hazard.

Medics were supposed to save people. They took that oath when they got officially certified as corpsmen, but they were also generally pretty good shots, having to train constantly for being in the middle of fighting. But if all the bugs got wiped out tomorrow, Miguelito would happily put the pistol away forever.

He opened his medkit and sprayed some disinfectant onto Ellis's wound and let it work its way in as the Eland slapped some cloth tape on the rip in his jacket. Wouldn't fix it but would keep it together until they could get back to a decent armorer.

Assuming they got back.

Ellis hissed with sudden pain, but that was good. Meant that the shock was wearing off. Everything looked good, so Miguelito got out the staple gun and the glue and closed the wound up, adding some special salve from a recipe his abuela, his grandmother, had taught him.

"You're good," he told the Eland gunman. "Anybody else get hit back there?"

He looked around. Strider Blue was still talking to Teela, the Grace scavenger who was supposed to open doors and security systems before the gunmen did. The boss looked a little rough around the edges, but he was a boffin, used to electronic systems and data cores, rather than actually walking onto a derelict looking for buried treasure, like they did in the old pirate stories.

Teela's headful of sensory tentacles were writhing and poking every which way right now, just like a mass of hungry, agitated snakes atop her head. People called the species Medusas as often as Grace, which was stupid, considering how cute the woman was otherwise.

And those tentacles let her sense all sorts of things the rest of the species in Kekik Space could only guess at. Or use electronic sensors.

Head shakes from everyone so Miguelito put his medkit away and watched Iron Scarab clean Three-Dub blood off her spear with a blue chamois. Looked like meditation, but she was scowling hard enough to maybe curdle milk.

The room they were in was small, more of like an airlock connecting two of those enormous cargo bays, since the hallway presumably continued. At least Teela had locked the door behind them and those bugs couldn't get in, short of ripping it down.

That just left the rest of the derelict for them to hide.

"We're lost right the moment," Strider announced, as if maybe the survivors hadn't already figured that part out. "Also, we are cut off from the place where the ship will dock for us, so we need to survive the next thirty-six hours until they return. Possibly, we will need to signal them from a different airlock at that point, but the ship coming for us is prepared for such an outcome. I had not expected anything to be this far forward on the derelict, or I would have come in from a hatch even further back. We are cut off and I'm not sure the best way to keep the rest of us alive."

Well, then. Succinct. Honest. Brutally straightforward.

Miguelito had always hoped that he was invincible and immortal. Several years of walking derelicts with various teams had maybe given him hope that he might be in that ten percent that got rich. As opposed to the fifty percent that never made it home.

Miguelito looked around at the little pseudo-family that any long-term adventuring group eventually turned into, even as he was still the outsider. Iron Scarab was a hard woman, even for an Eland. Ellis was quiet. Teela called herself a scavenger, but everyone understood that she was really a cat burglar who just happened to prey on dead ancients rather than the living out at Tooley's Station, or anywhere in the massive complex of ships, stations, and leftovers known as Dobson's Corner, hiding out in the cold depths of space.

Strider looked on the verge of panic. That would be bad. Miguelito decided that he needed to do something quick.

"Teela, nobody can open this door without an alarm going off, right?" Miguelito asked her carefully, trying to not get mesmerized by her tentacles. "Or the one in front of us?"

"Yes," the Grace woman nodded, her own voice a little shaky.

She was tiny, especially for a Grace, who tended to be Human sized. Not all that much taller than an Agama or a Mondi. Quiet, too, but that was occupational as much as anything.

"So, let's rest here," Miguelito continued. "Take an hour or so and maybe let the adrenaline burn off. Meditate a little. I'll fix us some food. Then we can move forward. How many cargo sections are ahead of us?"

Strider Blue's eyes focused on Miguelito now and he watched some of the madness recede from that Eland's mind. Medics were also pretty good psychologists, and Abuela had been the best ever at understanding how people ticked. How to heal them, both physically and emotionally. What to cook for them.

"The section ahead of us should be the forward-most one," Strider answered, his voice slowly gaining strength. "I think. The command deck should be above it and close to the front, based on the design of the vessel in the old Kekik records. This was one of their ships, before…"

The words trailed off.

Before.

Everyone used that term to describe the utopian paradise that supposedly existed before the Lapsyne came nearly a century ago.

"Before," Miguelito agreed, taking in the whole group in a moment of understanding that his Abuela would have called the second sight. "I'll work. You and Teela rest. Ellis, can you and Iron Scarab keep a loose watch?"

Everyone nodded and he got to work.

Miguelito had his doubts about Utopia, but now was not the time to express them. Nor was this the group.

Kekik jump-gates were organic things, powered by living minds. Literally, a sentient creature, according to what Miguelito had understood from certain books not many people ever read. A person in a nutrient bath, with all their limbs removed and their mind plugged permanently into a computer system that let them use their native or enhanced psionic powers to open a portal, a jump-gate, that let a ship travel instantly between stars.

The Kekik had supposedly many volunteers for such things in those days, at least according to the histories, since you were connected with every other mind in the network all the time and might live a thousand years.

Humans didn't have as much natural psionic power as the Kekik or the Grace, but there were supposedly at least a few jump-gates with Human masters, but nobody knew for sure.

Because the Kekik had found themselves a world somewhere. Old myths, only spoken and never written down, talked a lot more about it than the official histories.

The dominant native species hadn't had technology as anyone understood at the time. But they were a powerful psionic organism natively. Then the Kekik had amplified that by taking the type of Lapsyne now called a Siren and creating the thing called a queen.

Teotihuacan. The Spider Goddess of Mayan culture. At least as the memories of the Maya had been preserved down the generations getting into space and meeting the Kekik.

And four generations since the Lapsyne.

So much had been lost in the mad flight to escape the alien invasion. So many stories garbled. That was why the Eland, the Lost, had their own storytellers like the astronomers. To preserve the past.

The Spider Goddess could control minds. Human, Kekik, Bounder, Sabertooth, Eland. Anybody. Put enough queens together and their song became dominant. They'd only been defeated by Humans who'd been amplified by the Grace. The Cursed, as these defenders were called.

The Grace had created the Cursed. Only Humans were generally crazy enough. But they had managed to break the song of the Spider Goddess.

Miguelito had worked with a few people who had been rescued from Her cult. They were always a little crazy afterwards. Thankfully, nobody on this team.

Everyone settled and he dug his kitchen kit out of his backpack.

Abuela had taught Miguelito how to cook. Really cook, rather than just pull something from the freezer box and put it into the microwave for a certain period. Actual ingredients, from a hydroponics facility somewhere, grown and harvested, usually with love.

His team needed six seconds of courage.

That was what Abuela had called it. When things were threatening to get out of hand. To overwhelm you with grief and fear.

Six Seconds of Courage.

For her, it had come from food. Not just any food, though. Food prepared with love.

They needed Abuela's love right now.

Three Eland. A Grace. And one Human. They couldn't be sure where the air systems flowed to, but at least the atmosphere in here was good. Clean, in spite of perhaps running for more than a century without maintenance.

You never cooked on a derelict. Too much risk of the smell drawing Sirens, Three-Dubs, or crab tanks down on you.

He considered some ceviche right now from his supplies, but that was too bright a taste. They needed something darker on their palate to help them achieve calm.

He pulled out the rice cooker and added two cups of grains. Timer set and cooking. From another pouch, the seaweed wraps called nori. Five, because it would be a meal to brace them. Pickled cucumber and carrot already sliced into long, thin sticks. Herring steaks covered in avocado oil and sealed in plastic for need. Two of those came out as well.

Miguelito pulled his cutting sheet and his yanagiba knife and set out to make this meal memorable.

"Chumaki," Miguelito announced, presenting five rolls on his cutting board to the others with a bit of a flourish. Green mustard incorrectly called wasabi was mixed with a salty soya sauce for dipping in a small bowl.

They had been watching him work, and now greeting him with smiles as each reached out and took a disk of sliced sushi roll. As they began to dip it warmed his day.

"What is it?" Strider Blue asked as he looked up, the boffin having spent the last twenty minutes or so intently studying maps and architectural drawings on his abacus, the tablet computer and personal scanner device that translated out of Gringo as Escáner Personal.

S.P.

Time and a sense of humor had taken to naming such a device a Sancho Panza, after the ancient wisdom that A man setting out on an impossible quest needed to first locate his Sancho Panza to keep him safe.

"Six seconds of courage," Miguelito told them. "My abuela, my grandmother always believed that the secret to courage was good food. That when things got dangerous and bad, the memory of a special meal like this would carry you forward. You just needed to remember it to get those six seconds of courage."

"Does it work?" Iron Scarab asked in a hard voice that still managed to sound curious rather than derisive.

"It has so far," Miguelito replied, smiling at her as she crammed a disk into her mouth and chewed.

They ate in a companionable silence. Miguelito watched Abuela's magic work as Eland ears flickered forward again and shoulders lowered.

Medics were more than just staple guns and healing salves. They also brought chicken soup. He had a can stashed in his pack for a real emergency, but the maki was doing the job right now.

"So now what?" Ellis spoke up, his words a little slurred as he chewed.

"I think I know where we are," Strider replied, sounding far less confident than yesterday, but also maybe a little less arrogant as well.

"They have to know where we are," Iron Scarab said flatly. "Even with the locked door."

"There is a maintenance corridor we can access, just outside the hatch forward," Strider said. "That drops us under the cargo bay."

"I thought we wanted to go up?" Miguelito offered carefully, gauging the nerves around him.

"We do," Teela said. "The corridor intersects another corridor that gets us to either side, and then we can bypass most of the open space, assuming that the spiders are living in there."

"Corridor?" Iron Scarab asked. "How wide?"

"A little under three meters square," Strider replied. "We still use Human measurements for things instead."

"I'll lead," Iron Scarab announced. "Ellis, you'll protect the rear. Human, you'll stay close behind me with your pistol. I know you can use it and the other two are non-combatants."

"I can shoot," Teela snapped, gesturing to her own pistol.

"You will be listening," Iron Scarab snapped back, scowling and looking down her short snout at the Grace woman. "And watching. Miguelito can shoot until he has anything else to do. Professor, you'll follow behind her and ahead of Ellis."

Everybody nodded.

"Close in?" Miguelito asked the big Eland woman.

A nod, so he dug into his medical bag and pulled out a couple of vials. He mixed two into a third quickly and gave it a hard shake.

"Iron Scarab, you need to put this on your chest, arms, and spear," he told her, handing her the jar filled with greenish ooze.

"What is it?"

"A base," Miguelito explained. "It will neutralize acid if we run into a spitter or kill something that might splatter acid blood on you. They can sit back if they're smart and snipe at us. I just hope they don't have a nanny laying new eggs they can program as grenades."

"They aren't that smart," Strider scowled. "Nannies are only egg-layers."

"They understand threat," Miguelito corrected the man, firmly but still politely. "They react intelligently. In a tunnel, that would be grenades or a crabtank. She won't have time to hatch a tank or anything big, not if we're going to be gone in thirty-six hours, but they know grenades."

"Crab tank?" Teela asked.

"Some people call them razorbears," Ellis spoke up now. "Four massive legs to provide leverage for a lot of muscle and armor, and then two big pincers like a crab up front. They even go through powered armor."

"Oh," Teela said. "Them. Heard about them. Never seen one."

"Most people who see one don't last long enough to tell about it," Ellis said. "If we hadn't been running, I'd have grabbed heavier guns off Bullseye and Hunts, but we'll make do."

He put word to action and unslung his bolter rifle now. Like his pistol, it fired an oversized cartridge that was more like a small rocket, with a compact bursting charge on the tip designed to explode compactly as soon as it hit something. But they were soft tips, so they didn't go through bulkheads and maybe let all the atmosphere out, killing you like the idiots who insisted on armor-piercing ammunition for Lapsyne warriors and their chitinous hides.

Miguelito just had a simple pistol. Maybe a little better than Teela's or Strider's, but only because he'd trained with it so much. And tinkered with it as well. All specialists were rednecks at the end of the day. He might specialize in healing and buffing, but he'd spent enough time around armorers and mechanics to share a few secrets and learn a few things.

Iron Scarab had a spear for close in work, and a handful of short javelins she called plumbata. Heavy and designed to be thrown underhanded or sidearm, as well overhand like he would have.

Against Humans on the other side of any of these doors, smoke grenades or maybe something caustic or smelly might have been useful, but Lapsyne were masters of biology, and had regularly adapted their designs to overcome Human gimmicks, so people relied on firearms and cold steel.

Miguelito packed everything as they finished eating. Iron Scarab sprayed herself down with the oil that could help protect her against acid, then handed it back so he could do the same.

The others prepared in their own ways.

Ellis stepped close and nodded as Teela went to work on the lock, his bolter rifle up and ready. Miguelito drew his pistol and aimed it. The Professor stepped back into a corner back out of the way, even though he had a pistol out. As Iron Scarab said, he was no fighter.

Teela did something and the door beeped.

"Everyone ready?" she asked in a quiet voice.

Nods. She pushed a button and scurried back.

Miguelito didn't feel like a front-line shooter, but Hunts and Bullseye weren't here. Weren't coming back. He had to fill that slot for Ellis and Iron Scarab.

Six seconds of courage.

The door opened by sliding slowly, quietly into the wall.

Ellis fired a shot as soon as he had a space to stick the barrel of his bolter rifle, booming loudly in the confined space. Miguelito could only imagine what the sound would have been like if everyone wasn't wearing foam protectors stuffed down their ear canals.

The door continued open and Miguelito saw movement. He fired, assuming that there was nothing friendly out there. Even if it was Hunts or Bullseye, that would just mean that they had been captured and turned.

Sirens could do that, given time. Sing their song and warp your mind until you came to worship the queens.

That was the mistake the Blues had made. The queens had recruited almost as fast as they could sing and walk, killing anyone who resisted the song and eventually getting access to starships that could carry the infection through jump gates.

All planets were lost now. You couldn't clear a whole planetary surface simultaneously, except to bombard it to utter destruction and even then, you could only hope that you'd gotten them all.

Thank the gods who remained that only a queen could access a jump gate, and not any of the lesser breeds of warriors like Sirens or nannies. There had never been that many queens, and they didn't breed that fast. The Cursed had been able to track them down and break their song.

Eventually, all the species had adapted the potion and created their own versions of the curse. Drink this and you gain amazing, enormous mental power, until you went completely insane a few years later.

However, the figures in front of Miguelito were simple Three-Dubs, plus a pair of Renders, fast, two dimensional versions of the Three-Dub who just had slashing razors for all four hands and dewclaws on their legs. Dumb, fast, and lethal.

Ellis had started with one of those. Miguelito shot the other one, assuming that anything getting close now was Iron Scarab's responsibility.

Her spear flashed out and back like the tongue of a serpent, except that limbs tended to come off when she did that. Heads. Legs. Claws.

Six seconds of courage. Twelve seconds of mayhem. Bodies everywhere.

"Anybody hurt?" Miguelito looked around and tried to see everyone.

"No," Iron Scarab replied. She turned to Teela and scowled. "Move, little one."

The group stepped out of the small room and tried to look every direction at once. Miguelito was a step back from the front three, remembering how that first ambush had occurred when the Three-Dub dropped from overhead.

He kept glancing overhead.

Teela slid along the wall like a cat and dropped to her knees. Iron Scarab shifted to stand over the Grace like a mother bear. Strider Blue stepped close and everyone pointed guns outward as the scavenger worked.

Time had not been kind here. To Miguelito's eye, the gravity had flickered more than once over however long, causing some of these enormous containers to break loose from how they were normally locked down. They had instead floated a little randomly until gravity had come back on, eventually ending up in piles that looked like random collections of sticks.

Miguelito didn't know the particular model of ship they were on, but it had been one of the biggest ones. Twelve enormous bays, each roughly one hundred meters tall, three hundred and forty wide, and seventeen hundred long. Millions of shipping containers being hauled between worlds and systems on the day that a queen had emerged from a nearby jump gate and attacked this system.

You couldn't clear a planet once it had been infected, so the Humans in this system had annihilated it instead. Dobson was a cindered mess these days, after angry Humans had thrown large, iron rocks at it to explode in the lower atmosphere with shock waves bringing two-thousand-degree heat over enormous areas.

Death. Even for Lapsyne invaders who were worse than cockroaches that way.

Dobson's Corner was all that was left, a collection of stations and ships way out in the cold darkness and hidden. Several million people, with just over half of them Human. Miguelito had grown up on the section known as Tooley's Station, and always hoped he'd manage to retire there someday.

Nothing emerged from the jumble as he watched.

Teela cursed vile enough for Miguelito to consider blushing for her.

"It's jammed," she said.

"What do you mean, jammed?" Iron Scarab asked, never taking her eyes off their surroundings.

"It's unlocked, but I can't get it to open," the Grace woman said.

"Human," Iron Scarab called, getting Miguelito's attention. "Cover me."

Are you nuts?

But he didn't say that out loud. He Who Hunts and Bullseye were dead, or they would have done that job. One Human specialist corpsman was all the Eland woman had right now with Ellis covering the other flank.

He nodded and stepped further to his right, paranoia drawing his eyes every which way.

From the sound, Iron Scarab had put her spear and plumbata down. He heard her hooves settle on the deck and rock back a little so her boots could grip.

Eland footwear was always interesting. They had hooves and liked those clear but wore a thing that covered the sensitive rear and wrapped their fetlocks to protect them. Iron Scarab went colorful with hers, bright blue and gold patterns, while Ellis's were a simple gray.

Iron Scarab growled and cursed.

Miguelito wanted to watch, but he and Ellis had to cover the entire emptiness of the bay. They had maybe forty meters to the edge of the closest pile. More than any Three-Dub could cover before somebody got a shot off.

Hopefully.

Miguelito's great fear now was that a nanny had started laying weapon eggs for her warriors. Or worse, had a stash already laid and waiting, that just needed to be activated.

Web-throwers, hurling eggs that exploded into a sticky mess across a space of deck to capture you. Or web-bolters that just hit one person and spun them up like spiders. Or exploding grenades that fired chitinous shrapnel everywhere.

Thank the gods that the nanny hadn't prepared a spitter or a manticore waiting for them out here, to say nothing of a dragon.

At least so far.

Miguelito didn't see any movement. The sound of metal seemingly tearing behind him hopefully presages success.

"It is open," Iron Scarab announced. "Human, you come with me into the hole while the others prepare to join us."

If Nannies understood Spanish, that would be their cue to attack, as soon as the party was divided. Miguelito still didn't see any movement.

Didn't mean nobody was watching. Just meant that maybe the nanny had come up with a plan and needed to know which way her next victims were headed.

Iron Scarab took the Eland by the horns and jumped right down into the hole with an enormous crashing sound.

"Now," she called, and Miguelito flipped his safety on and jumped sideways after her.

It was lit down here. Again, the ship somehow knew where the crew was and did things with ancient, electronic magic that the moderns could not replicate.

She was faced one way, so Miguelito turned the other and aimed at the empty corridor, flipping his safety back off to shoot at someone.

Anyone.

Everyone.

Nobody rushed out of the distant dimness.

"Everyone now," Iron Scarab called. "Professor first, then Teela, then Ellis Glenraven."

Miguelito stepped forward a little, enough to realize that the corridor went a short distance and turned.

"I have a blind corner," he announced in that calm emotionless voice scouts and shooters practiced. "Approaching to cover."

"Exercise care, Human," Iron Scarab called. "You might be the most important person now."

He started to argue with her categorically but subsided before the words reached his mouth. They weren't exploring the derelict now such much as trying to stay ahead of the infestation of bugs.

To stay alive.

Strider Blue knew the architecture. Teela handled locks. The other two killed.

Only Miguelito could keep folks alive when the battles were over.

He moved to the outer edge of the hallway and pointed his pistol, ready to fire at anything. The lights were on, but that was an automated function of the system detecting movement down here.

Could have been him. Could have been spiders coming from the other end.

He got to the corner and nobody was crouched around it, hiding from him.

"Clear this direction," he said loud enough for the others.

Strider Blue landed heavily. Teela came down like a cat.

Ellis waited a long beat and then hopped down onto his stomach, pulling the plate back into place as he dropped.

Maybe nobody would know where they'd gone.

A guy could hope, right?

Teela did something and the overhead beeped again.

"Should be locked," she said quietly.

"Assist the Human," Iron Scarab announced. "Professor, you as well."

Miguelito watched the two approach out of the corner of his eye, never losing the dimness, in case he picked up distant movement.

Both of the newcomers peeked around the corner and then slid back and whispered. Iron Scarab moved close and Ellis stayed at the far end of the corridor, just under the hatch, in case someone opened it right now.

Something.

Bullseye and Hunts were gone. Dead, hopefully, rather than taken.

At least the Lapsyne didn't lay eggs in living tissue, like some Human insects. They either took your mind or ate your flesh, depending.

Shoot first. Apologize to the ghosts of any sentients later.

Iron Scarab nodded to him and moved quickly across his line of fire to the far side of the corridor, where she could also watch.

"Okay," Strider said. "This is the access way I expected. We go this way and about a third of the way down there will be an intersection we can take. Either side will get us to a stairwell we can ascend."

Miguelito had never been on a derelict this big, so he didn't know. But the Kekik, those damned Blues who had started it all, had built mammoth ships. Made sense that you'd want ways to move around that weren't in a bay, in case you had to vent it to space, or turn the gravity off to move things around.

Iron Scarab took that nasty spear in one hand with all her plumbata except one. She carried that one for a snap throw if something jumped out.

She turned that sugar skull to face him and Miguelito felt a deathly chill. Like someone had walked across his grave. It didn't help that she had spiraled both her horns with white paint and added fine red stripes and designs over that, like blood dripping down her horns.

He wondered if there were any of the bugs that might be intimidated at that woman's scowl. It would be a shame to waste it, because she was one amazingly badass warrior babe right now and seemed to project those pheromones all over the group.

He certainly felt better. Her scowl would keep him going, as would those six seconds of courage from the meal.

"We move," she announced, stepping off and remaining to the left, with him to the right.

Teela and the boffin came next behind him as he followed her. Miguelito didn't look back but assumed Ellis kept a space.

The air down here had a thick, almost chewy taste to it. Hopefully, that meant that the Lapsyne didn't come down here that often, if ever. A few of the light strips down here were burned out. That surprised him. Miguelito couldn't remember the last ship he had been on with burned out light bulbs.

Dim, sure. Yellowing with age, frequently. But actually, burned out? Man, those must be old.

Still, it was bright enough that nobody was going to sneak up on them. He just hoped that the nannies out there never figured out how to do something like a chameleon, birthing new Three-Dubs or something that could change the color or texture of their chitin to hide as they snuck up on you.

They would make it nearly impossible to try to clear a derelict. You'd be better off at that point just venting everything to space. Pain in the ass, because everyone would have to upgrade from the emergency skinsuits, they usually wore with rebreathers handy. No, you'd have to be in full cargo suits or maybe even exoframes to do the job.

In the distance, Miguelito saw that dangerous intersection coming closer. Nobody straight ahead, but two side corridors that could hide things.

Monsters. Killers.

Iron Scarab signaled for the others to remain behind, but motioned Miguelito to put his butt against the corridor across from her so they could slide down and watch each way.

And each other.

Not that the Eland warrior was hard on the eyes. He'd known some people who took their specism in weird directions. Miguelito shrugged and took another step.

Eland were erect biped humanoids. More or less. Taller and wider than Humans, on average. Covered over with a thin fur he'd heard compared to horses, but he'd never seen such a creature to tell.

They walked in a manner similar to if Miguelito was up on his toes, in the Eland's case with that last joint covered over by a fused hoof. They had long calves and short thighs, kind of like a cat walking upright. Hands with three fingers instead of four, and blunt nails that didn't grow all that much.

It was the head that really marked her as alien. Two horns spiraling out of the sides of her forehead and up to points. Wide eyes that apparently let them see in the dark as well. Short snouts that looked like cattle, if you squinted at both pictures.

She caught him staring at her and one eyebrow went up, even as neither ear twitched from where she had them pointed forward.

Stop daydreaming.

He slid along, listening. Smelling. Hoping.

Nothing emerged into his line of sight. She didn't suddenly explode into lethal violence.

Miguelito let go the breath he had been holding and nodded at Iron Scarab.

She might have grinned at him, but it was gone before he was sure.

"Come," she signaled the others quietly.

Teela and the Professor got close. Miguelito and the two Eland watched four approaches simultaneously with their faces outward.

"This way," Strider said after a moment of consultation with the scavenger.

"Same pattern as before," Iron Scarab said, moving into the new corridor.

Miguelito fell in and watched her move, wondering if there was a stubby tail in there under her pants as her bottom occasionally distracted him.

Stay on focus!

They got a little ahead of the others now, by design. Scouting for the others as they crossed the width of the bay above them.

"Human, do you hear that?" she whispered.

Miguelito paused and focused. Teela was the one with the best eyes and ears. And sensory tentacles on her head.

But she was back with the Professor.

He listened.

It wasn't a sound. Or rather, you didn't hear it with your ears.

He'd dreaded that call, every time he had ever set foot on a derelict, station or ship.

The Song of the Spider Goddess.

They weren't just facing a Nanny and her brood, but an actual Siren. The original leaders of the Lapsyne, before the Blues had genetically engineered those Queens who had proven to be their undoing.

Everyone's undoing.

Her call wormed its way into his head, but he growled and pushed it out somehow.

He glanced back and gestured to the others that he had heard something. Ellis nodded. Teela began to hyperventilate, from the look of her. The Professor paled under his fur.

The sound of a spear hitting the deck snapped Miguelito's head around. Iron Scarab's plumbata landed a moment later and she staggered a step forward.

Shit, she'd been taken. Called into servitude to the queens.

At a minimum, she would run to them now and be eaten. Worse, she might survive long enough to tell the bugs where to find the invaders.

She staggered a second step forward, gathering herself now as her brain stopped being her own.

Miguelito had one chance to do something. And even trying might get him killed.

If he didn't, though, the rest of them were probably just as doomed.

He holstered his pistol and took off after her as she began to move faster.

Hopefully, that sound was penetrating deck plates, rather than the Lapsyne being down here in the tunnel with them, just ahead where he was about to run right into a hunting party.

Do, or die.

She got stopped by a closed panel. If he was counting his steps right, they had both come to the edge of the bay and her brain wasn't coherent enough right now to work the control panel on the right, green blinking at both of them as a reminder.

He clenched both hands and stepped right up behind the Eland woman, wondering if this was the dumbest thing he had ever done.

Six seconds of courage. Abuela had always told him that those six seconds could make all the difference in the world.

He reached up with a hand and pinched her ear. On an Eland, they could go from horizontal, stuck out sideways, to upright, turned either forward or backward depending on need and mood

They were stuck out sideways right now.

He squeezed it between two fingers enough to get her attention, but not to damage the ear itself.

"Iron Scarab, wake up," he called.

She did. Or rather, her training and instincts took over. She was as old as Ellis, long time drinking buddies but nothing more. Combat veterans going back decades. Dangerous, dangerous woman.

She spun with an elbow and knocked his hand away.

Miguelito already knew what was coming next, so he let go easy enough and grabbed at those painted horns as she lowered them and got ready to gore him.

Instinct. A lethal and irresistible thing. So much stronger than this Eland woman's waking brain.

She drove with her legs, lifting Miguelito up and slamming him into the side of the corridor with pain-maddened eyes.

"Iron Scarab, fight them," he called weakly, almost all the breath driven from his lungs by the impact. "Six seconds of courage. You are stronger than she is."

Iron Scarab growled with rage and tried again to drive him through the metal wall.

"Remember my abuela and the magic of good food with your friends," Miguelito said, his voice slowly returning. "Love and cooking."

She blinked. Or rather, the other creature blinked, and Iron Scarab was there in her eyes afterwards.

"Human?" she asked, anger and confusion at war with one another.

"Spider Goddess," Miguelito said with what was left us his breath. "She's calling you. You must resist her."

Iron Scarab shook her head. Miguelito got bounced around because he refused to let go of those horns, so close to gutting him like one of his fish.

She blinked again and smiled wryly.

"You are crazy, Human," she said. "Has anyone told you that?"

"A few people."

"Not many would choose to wrestle with an Eland," Iron Scarab lowered her head stepped back. Miguelito's feet finally landed on the deck again as he let go of her horns. "Fewer would survive."

"Without you, we're all dead," Miguelito said. "It was worth the risk."

She smiled and stepped fully clear.

Miguelito glanced back, but the others were tiny in the distance. Probably sure that both of them had been taken by now. Ellis would likely open fire on them if they walked back that way now.

"She is just outside this door," Iron Scarab pointed to the closed hatch. "Calling me still, but thanks to you and your abuela I can resist her."

She looked back at the others and came to the same conclusion as Miguelito did.

"We must kill her," the Eland woman said.

Miguelito nodded. He was surprised when Iron Scarab reached into one of her pouches and pulled out a heavy pistol.

"I trained with the spear," she grinned at him. "But I can use most weapons."

"How many are there?" he asked, wondering what information that song had conveyed.

"A few," Iron Scarab said. "She had sent most of her warriors to cover the other exits from this warren. Nobody could resist her."

She scowled at him accusingly, but Miguelito shrugged.

"My abuela was a good witch," he offered.

Those were her words, whenever he had come down with a cold or something, she then proceeded to heal with chicken soup or cookies.

He was one of the lucky ones. Most of the children who got orphaned by the wars were raised in crèches, but one set of his grandparents had survived to raise him.

"Let us use her magic, then, Human," Iron Scarab stepped to the door and charged her pistol.

Miguelito drew his and took a deep breath. He nodded to her and one long, fur-covered hand reached out and pushed the button.

The hatch opened.

The Song of the Spider Goddess was so loud Miguelito thought he might actually be able to record it for a scientist back home, but it was all in his mind.

Six Seconds of Courage.

He turned and shot the first thing that moved on the other side of the door.

Siren.

Two meters and change tall. Instead of four arms, it had four long tentacles waving as though in a breeze. She was standing right there, facing him with all four eyes, the two big hunting ones and the two side ones that let her see all directions. Blue fur with orange stripes was a new color pattern to him, but he'd never actually seen a live one before.

The smell...

His brain kept wanting to translate her song into abuela's apple pie, fresh from the over, but he resisted it. Focused.

Underneath, there was a stink like wet dog. It wasn't, but that was the closest thing his brain could find to compare it in that moment of madness.

The creature seemed to blink at him as he pulled his trigger. Again. Again. Again.

Something ran into him from the side and Miguelito concentrated on not losing his pistol, even as the blow had been harder than Iron Scarab's and knocked him to the ground

Claws rolled him over and Miguelito looked up into the face of a Three-Dub, just about to open his stomach up like a surgeon.

The creature's head exploded, spraying green acid blood everywhere.

Iron Scarab put a second shot into the creature for good measure and then pivoted, emptying her magazine.

Standing might take too much time, so Miguelito just rolled onto his side and fired. The Siren was only now falling over, but she had gone silent and he could think again.

Another creature nearby made it to a flight of stairs, but he managed to hit her. It. That thing.

Nanny. Mother of monsters.

His shot caught her in the back, just about dead center like when you were on a target range. She staggered.

Miguelito felt the click as his magazine was empty.

Where had all the bullets gone?

The Nanny rose, bleeding, and started up the steps again.

Miguelito went into a fugue. He didn't have any other term for it.

The entire universe came down to him and that wounded Nanny.

If she got away, she would lay more eggs and hatch another generation of monsters to hunt them. She would find the ones already racing forward from the other directions to get Ellis and the others.

He rose to a knee like an automaton.

Iron Scarab was killing things around him, but that was a different universe.

One thumb down to drop the magazine. Catch it with your free hand and extract it.

Drop the hand down and slam the empty into a pouch.

Pull the next one free.

Reverse your motion and slam it home. Rack the slide to chamber the next bullet.

She had one claw on a door controller, pushing.

In a moment it will open, and she will escape you.

Then you will die.

Miguelito let the gods of Humanity and Eland guide his shot to strike down the terrible avatar of the spiders.

One shot. Her head exploded in a green spray as the door opened.

Miguelito fell back into real time and looked around him at the carnage.

Dead Siren. Dead nanny. Many dead Three-Dubs apparently caught by surprise when the song failed.

Miguelito rose.

Iron Scarab looked at him and nodded.

Just that, but in conveyed a wealth of value. Of acceptance.

The two of them had done it.

Alone.

He dug into his pack and found the tactical radio they rarely used.

"Ellis, this is Miguelito," he said quietly, unsure if there were other monsters around.

"Status?" the other Eland replied.

"We killed the ambush," he said, a little breathless at the number of dead bodies around them. "Siren. Nanny. Three-dubs. More are coming at you from the other three directions, but if we move now, we should be able to get to the bridge ahead of them and seal ourselves in for now."

"That would be acceptable," the Professor was suddenly on the line. "There is an airlock from there we should be able use to escape."

"You okay?" Ellis asked.

"Ask me again in a week," Miguelito said, unsure.

Iron Scarab smiled but didn't comment. He closed the radio and waited.

At the top of those stairs, the hatch had closed again when the Nanny died. She was slowly tumbling backwards down the stairs, lifeless, as he watched.

Footsteps approached from behind. Miguelito holstered his pistol and held his hands out sideways as Ellis came into sight, hiding behind that enormous bore of his bolter rifle.

"Shit, Miguelito," the Eland warrior said with something that sounded like awe in his voice. "You two did this?"

"He did most of the damage," Iron Scarab broke her silence. "I merely killed some Three-Dubs while he slaughtered the rest."

Miguelito turned to stare at her in surprise.

She smiled disarmingly at him and stepped close. Suddenly, he was engulfed in a hug.

"Thank you, Miguelito," she said quietly. "My name is Janeta. Welcome to the family."

Sometimes Salvation Slithers

Cynthia A. Knoble

Todd had to fart but didn't dare. It wasn't the fellow passengers lined up with him to pass through the security gate in the airport terminal that caused him to hold the fart in. It was the package inside him. He might not blow it out his ass but couldn't be sure. He wiped nervous sweat from his brow. Usually, he was cool as a cucumber going through customs. The fear of being caught and jailed didn't scare him. His life was in a downspin. No, it was swirling the bowl already so jail couldn't be any worse. He didn't care about the risks of being a drug mule. Drugs would kill him eventually so did it matter if he died from a ruptured condom in his belly or from a needle between his toes?

This particular run though was wrong. The package was huge, and he hadn't swallowed it as he normally did. His contacts rammed quite a large package up his ass after he refused to do so himself. His asshole stung and it hurt to sit down. His past girlfriends were troopers. Then again, he had always prepared them well, never just rammed his dick up there.

The line inched closer to the gate. The drug-sniffing dog there eyed Todd with suspicion. It couldn't smell drugs inside his body and his colon should be as much protection as his stomach but was it? He wiped away more sweat as his turn arrived. The guard's expression matched that of the dog as he scanned Todd's passport. There was a lot of activity on it, but Todd had been careful, visiting countries other than the known drug-producing ones. He had a cover story if needed, how he was a locations scout for a film production company. His boss had even given him a special number that would be answered by an employee of the fake company, but he had never had to employ the cover story. Young men travelling on their own used to scream drug mule to the authorities but as the men were targeted, traffickers turned to women, usually in groups, more likely to be seen as tourists. When the authorities caught onto that, women were also under suspicion. With older, sometimes elderly mules on the rise, no one was currently beyond suspicion, but no specific group was targeted any longer.

The guard handed back the passport and urged Todd through with an impatient wave of his hand. Relieved at having that ordeal behind him, Todd made his way to the waiting area of the appropriate gate. He stood, his small and only bag between his splayed feet, not eager to sit. His cab ride to the airport had not been pleasant.

Once on the plane, he tried to find comfort in his seat, but his ass was tender. He also needed to shit but should not have to, considering he hadn't eaten. He never did before accepting a package, just in case the flight was delayed and his ability to shit at home was compromised. After a torturous several hours of holding in a shit during his first, nerve-racked run, he had learned much. He was old hat at smuggling, never breaking a sweat over his runs any longer. Well, until today and the enormous package currently up his poop-chute.

Couriering drugs was a far cry from his college days of only a few years ago. He studied English literature (really, what had he expected to do with that degree?) and struggled to maintain his grades. He needed a little something to help him keep up with school and his part-time job. Booze wasn't cutting it, coke was too expensive, and weed made him too chill to work. His anxiety had him losing weight and sleep. Enter heroin. Dirty but cheap. He didn't believe trying heroin once would be as addictive as he had heard. Well, colour him stupid because an addict was born that night, one who would do anything for a hit. School was long gone, along with his family and friends. Being sticky-fingered in people's homes caused them to forbid him from coming around again. Enter Dumps, a dealer with an offer. And so, Todd was a mule, not proud of his actions but supplied with heroin all the same.

He wasn't presently carrying H though. He had never seen it packaged like that, and not swallowing it didn't sit well with him either. It had sort of looked like a butt plug only without a stopper on the end. And it was huge. Sure, rectums stretched but fuck those guys. What they stuffed in him was fucking enormous. He was lucky his asshole didn't split. The package looked like plastic and was dark. He also swore he saw fluid moving in it. What the fuck had they put in him? *What does it matter? Just get home, get it out of you, and deliver it to Dumps. And tell that fucker you want more this time. This run is bullshit.* Yeah, sure, that's what he should tell Dumps, but he wouldn't. He would start to but when Dumps argued, Todd would give up as he always did. Because when it came down to it, all that mattered was the needle and by the time he saw Dumps, his need for it would be so intense it would obliterate every bit of reason he possessed, every bit of fight that might be left in him. He had stopped rationalizing his addiction long ago. Nothing of past-Todd remained. There was only addict-Todd, who loved holding the Devil's hand and reaching for that needle. He would suck the Devil's dick if need be.

Addict-Todd managed to act like a normal passenger, thanked the flight attendant for the water bottle she gave him and looked out the window from his aisle seat. There was no one in the window seat and the plane was filled to half-capacity. From his limited vantage point, Todd spotted a middle-aged couple two rows up from him who chatted with one another, and the backs of a few more heads. It was just as well. If it remained this quiet, he could nap. He settled himself as well as his burning asshole would allow, closed his eyes, and was asleep in no time.

About an hour later, according to his phone, he was sweating again. Great globs of it beaded his forehead and leaked down his temples. He had awoken to a terrifying feeling, a ping against the delicate flesh of his rectum but only on one side. The package inside him had ruptured, he was certain of it. He held his breath, waiting for the feel of a sharp edge plastic cutting him. It didn't come but something else did. A wetness between his cheeks, like he'd let loose a rip-roaring wet fart. The container was leaking.

He rose to his feet with caution, ready for the broken container to tear him open. When it didn't, he employed careful steps to the washroom. Once inside, he slid the lock in place and dropped his pants. There was a small stain on his underwear. Fuck this. He squatted over the bowl and pushed. The container might shred his ass, but he wanted it out of him. He winced as he forced it downward, his inner muscles working overtime to dispel the massive package. A clink of plastic against metal signaled his success, as did the increased burning of his hole which felt stretched wide enough to drive a truck through.

The container had ruptured all right, there was a long crack down one side of it, and a bit of blue liquid in the bottom. Along with the small spot on his underwear, that meant the majority of the liquid was still inside him. What the fuck was in it? Was he about to overdose? He knew guys who stuck vodka-soaked tampons up their asses to 'pre-drink' before parties. Gross, but it got them drunk fast, although a couple of them had ended up in the hospital with alcohol poisoning.

Jittery as all hell, Todd waited to see what would happen, even as there wasn't much to be done at thirty-five-thousand feet in the sky. His pulse was racing but he had just squeezed a giant container out his ass. His heart rate wasn't fast enough to signal an overdose and he wasn't drowsy. A glance in the mirror told him his pupils were normal. There was no bluish tinge to his fingernails or lips, and he felt as if he were breathing normally. Sure, he was a bit paranoid, but he had an unknown liquid inside him, in an area that readily absorbed what was in it. But he wasn't exhibiting any signs of an overdose, so that was good. His guts were squirming but that was just nerves. Only wait ... they were *actually* squirming.

Something was moving inside him. Snakes, no, too small. *Motherfucking snakes on a motherfucking plane.* He would laugh if he wasn't certain he was filled with living organisms. Should he say something? Was there an air marshal on board? Todd had read somewhere that less than one percent of all flights had a marshal on the plane. Their presence was based on risk-assessments. Still, this flight originated in Mexico, so there could be one onboard, but what would the marshal do? He certainly wouldn't believe Todd, let alone be able to do anything to help. *Fuck, fuck, fuckfuckfuck.* What was he supposed to do?

He wiped his ass, grimacing at the blue stain on the paper, and flushed the toilet. The container got caught lengthwise and bobbed in the flow of water that swirled under it. Todd turned it on its end and flushed again. As soon as the metal trapdoor opened, the container disappeared. The evidence of his smuggling was gone but what the fuck was inside him? *Dumps is gonna be pissed.*

Fuck Dumps. There was something alive inside Todd, something that squirmed. He discarded his underwear but not before inspecting it. The stain was dark blue and stank, like sewage and rotting potatoes. He washed his hands and returned to his seat.

He sat rigidly. The armpits and back of his shirt were wet with the sweat that poured from him. He swiped his forearm over his face. It was soaked. The squirming within him intensified, as if whatever the things were grew in size. There were so many of them. They traveled upwards, like bad gas bubbles but in the wrong direction. *The worms crawl in/the worms crawl out/the worms are tunneling through my guts.* He stifled a manic giggle. Worms was a good enough description for they felt like worms. And they were getting bigger. They were nightcrawlers now, working their way upwards. The movement stopped as they reached his stomach. Would the acid there kill them? With any luck, yes. Shitting out a huge pile of worms was disgusting but better than the alternative of them continuing their upwards trek.

Todd slumped in his seat. His butt hurt with his shift in position, but his relief overshadowed it. He pictured the invaders squiggling in pools of acid, dying. They should perish in no time considering there was no food in his stomach to compete with the worms for the acid's attention. Dumps might be pissed when he found himself empty-handed but fuck him for using Todd to smuggle whatever the hell those worms were into the country. What the fuck had Dumps got mixed up in? That greedy bastard would sell out his own mother so sacrificing Todd wouldn't faze him in the least.

This wouldn't be the wake-up call it should be. Todd would simply dodge Dumps while he sought out a new dealer. He might be an addict, but he had a profitable skill set now, one he could market. Hell, he could finagle a much better deal than his standing one with Dumps.

His entrepreneurial thoughts came to an end with the tickle of movement north of his stomach. His invaders had not succumbed to his stomach acid. One, two, more, many more wriggling up his ... esophagus? Probably. Not that he paid much attention in biology. Would he be able to breathe as those things made their way up? They felt like they were getting bigger again. They clung to his flesh as they propelled themselves upward, crawling through his chest.

Panic set in as breathing became an issue. He sucked air through his nostrils but not much. They were in his throat and triggered his gag reflex. He shot out of his seat and staggered to the washroom, grabbing at seatbacks as he made his way, lightheaded with the lack of oxygen. The washrooms were occupied. He would never make it to the next ones. He retched and covered his mouth with a hand. Something squirmed against his palm.

The flight attendant rushed to him with an air-sick bag. He snatched it from her and unloaded into it. Something slithered between his fingers as he gripped the bag. Disgusted noises sounded from nearby passengers but the flight attendant gasped. She had seen the worms, but Todd couldn't do anything about it. He could still barely breathe, and he was going to be sick again. The smell wafting from the bag didn't help. It literally smelled like shit. His next purge was heavier, and the bag moved with the many writhing bodies within it. One crawled into his nasal passages. It fucking hurt and he dropped the bag. As the worm made its appearance in his nostril, drawing tears from him, he grabbed the end of it and pulled. It resisted as countless pairs of tiny feet clung to his flesh. He yanked hard. The flight attendant screamed as he withdrew a ten-inch creature from his nose, gagging all the while.

It was indigo with lighter, shimmery streaks of blue and purple. When it wrapped around his wrist, Todd flung his hand to rid himself of the feel of dozens of teeny feet grabbing his skin. The worm flew and hit a female passenger in the face, one half of the couple Todd spotted earlier. Her scream was echoed by the flight attendant. The passenger's husband grabbed the worm, but it clung to her hair and lifted her hairspray-glued bangs. She screamed again. The man pulled and the worm released his wife's hair and wrapped around his wrist. He knocked it to the floor where he crushed it under his shoe. A horrendous smell filled the air, dank and noxious, with notes of excrement and decomposition.

Enraged, the man shoved Todd and stomped on the sick bag. The stench was unbearable and moans, retches, and further shrieks filled the air. On his ass, which gave a nasty jolt of pain on contact, Todd saw the first crushed worm. Half of it still wriggled. Could it live like that, as flatworms could? That was something he did remember from biology class. You could cut a flatworm into twenty pieces and each piece would live as a separate entity.

As the man's foot lifted off the bag, several unharmed worms leapt into the air and landed on the man's shoe. *Oh fuck, they practically flew!* Todd's mouth dropped open. What the serious fuck were these things? In a second, they were on the man's pant leg and a few wriggled under it. The man swatted at his leg as if it were on fire as Todd scrambled out of the way of fleeing passengers headed for the front of the plane. Through the blur of passing bodies, Todd kept his eyes on the man who tore his pant leg open. A worm was wriggling into his leg, its head no longer visible. A trickle of blood ran down his calf. More worms joined the party, as if encouraged by the screams in the air. Some could only move half their bodies, others less than that, but they targeted the man as if aware it was, he who had attacked them.

Another thunderbolt of nausea had Todd bringing up worms he was unaware had remained within him. He heaved with such intensity he shot the worms out in a high arc. They changed direction in mid-air to target the man's wife and flight attendant. The pair screeched as they batted at themselves.

Chaos surrounded Todd. People ran and screamed, worms were everywhere and some of them were growing again. Had he really thrown up that many of them? They varied in size so perhaps some may have been too small to see when he expelled them and had grown in the open air. They crawled and jumped and found passengers. Shrieks from ahead of Todd and behind him announced the worms had made their way through the body of the plane. The passengers Todd could see squealed as they tried to pluck worms off them but were covered in too many. The worms found nostrils and ears and mouths. Many broke skin and entered bodies that way.

Some passengers convulsed. Other people writhed in pain and moaned. A few ran as they held their heads or bellies. So much screaming everywhere. Todd clamped his hands over his ears but couldn't close his eyes. The terrible sights intrigued him as much as they disgusted him. While the people were frenzied, the worms seemed to have a plan. Two remained on Todd but didn't seem that interested in him.

In slow increments, the noise wound down as did the passengers. They all looked dead to Todd. The worms continued to crawl over bodies and under skin. Would the pilots, not able to raise flight attendants, come out? Todd didn't think so. They were safe in the enclosed cockpit.

Perhaps not having word from the body of the plane, they would have police on standby at the airport. What would the cops make of Todd, the only one not infected by the worms?

The worm on Todd's forearm was now the length of it and about two inches wide. He thought it was the same worm that had been between his fingers when he threw up in the bag, the first worm to exit him, the one that had squirmed against his palm before he barfed. Its many pairs of legs were visible now, short with tiny feet that resembled pincers. They held onto his skin but didn't pinch. With those feet, he supposed they weren't actually worms but their bodies were worm-like, albeit with stubby antennae like those on slugs. The one on his arm was a royal purple and not the indigo of the one he had pulled from his nose. The worm snaked around his ankle was forest green. Each sported streaks of jewel-tone colour. They were actually kind of beautiful.

"Are you going to hurt me?" he asked the one on his arm.

Its head reared up. It didn't have eyes but seemed to focus on Todd, nonetheless. Its antennae wriggled as it rubbed its head against his shoulder. Was that some kind of affectionate motion or was it tasting him in some way? He risked touching it. The worm's skin was soft and not slimy as he expected. It felt like a small snake and was warmer than he thought it could be. He ran his fingertip down the length of it, careful to be gentle. The worm rubbed its head against his shoulder and wiggled its antennae again.

In time, the bodies in the cabin swelled and bloated. Everywhere he looked Todd saw bloody holes where the worms had gained entry. They had penetrated arms and legs, chests and bellies. Faces had not escaped their rampage. The flight attendant had a hole in one temple and another in a cheek. Her skin rippled with movement underneath it. Were they eating the people from the inside out, or doing something else? They were growing, that was a certainty for the ones on Todd had grown again.

He tensed as the worm on his arm crawled higher. Draped over his shoulder, it rubbed his head against his neck then stayed in its new position, seemingly comfortable. Its back end extended past Todd's elbow. The one on his ankle had grown long enough to circle his calf as well.

The ring of a cellphone broke the silence. There could only be one person who didn't set their phone to airplane mode for the flight. Todd followed the sound, taking careful steps to not bother his worm passengers, and discovered the air marshal. Squirming movement under the man's cheeks and forehead were the work of much smaller worms than the ones on Todd. The worms were breeding. The passengers had become incubators.

Todd eyed the gun, in a holster at the man's side, exposed as he was slumped against seats, his jacket open. He could take the gun and do away with himself. It would be better than death by worms. The one on his shoulder was on the move again. Todd sucked in a breath as it crawled up his neck and over his jaw. Its head nudged his cheek, as if to assure him he was safe from them. Todd was worm-master, bringer of the plague although he didn't master the worms and he hadn't started the horror that killed all the passengers. *You* did *start all this. You barfed up the worms.* Well, that was true, but he couldn't control them. Or could he?

He glanced down a bit cross-eyed at the worm head reared up from his cheek. Its mouth was closed, a line across the bottom of its eyeless head, the edges pulled up at the corners as if smiling.

"Sit on my head," he told it. The way it wriggled its antennae was kinda cute. Todd held his breath as it crawled over his face, a mass of tiny feet gently grabbing at his nose, eyelid, and forehead as it rose. When it reached his head, he felt it curl up and nestle into his hair. *Fuck me. It listened to me.*

"Hey, you. The one on my leg," Todd called, glancing down but keeping his head steady to not jar his new friend. The worm wrapped around his ankle tilted its head up at him. "Curl up on my shoe." It did.

Fucking-A. He was Willard but with worms instead of rats. Ignoring Willard's film-demise, Todd furthered his worm-control. "You, on my shoe. Your name is B— Herman." He had almost said 'Ben' but remembered Ben was the trouble-making rat. He gently stroked the worm on his head. "Your name is Socrates." That was safe enough. Socrates was the nice rat. Todd had seen Willard as a child and had been scared shitless by it, but he now understood the story on a whole new level.

"Both of you should sit on my shoulders. It'll be safer when I walk around. C'mon, I'll get you guys a treat."

Socrates crawled to one shoulder as Herman slithered up Todd's leg and side to the other one. Todd made his way to where the flight attendant had emerged with the drink cart earlier. There would be food, too, as dinner was scheduled on the flight. Todd wouldn't have eaten had the flight proceeded in a normal fashion, but its new course found him famished. He found the food trays, already in the convection oven. Perfect. He pulled out a few. They were overcooked, close to burning. He shut off the oven and found utensils. He tried all the offerings available, rice, noodles, beef, chicken, vegetables, but the worms were only interested in the meat. As his stomach growled, Todd fed Socrates and Herman tiny bits of meat, watching as they devoured the morsels. They had large mouths when opened, filled with rows of needle-like teeth but they took the meat from between Todd's thumb and finger with a surprising gentleness.

Three more worms joined them, two green and one indigo, slithering up to the small counter Todd stood before. They waited, their sweet little antennae twitching, as Todd prepared small chunks of meat for them. As they ate, Todd dubbed the newcomers Delilah, Mick, and Stephen. He had no idea where those names came from but what did it matter? The worms responded to the names and enjoyed the meat. Before Todd's eyes, all five grew again. When they refused more meat, Todd ate, gobbling down three trays of food.

Full, he invited the newcomers to join Socrates and Herman. With his shoulders occupied, Delilah chose the top of his head and wrapped around it like a turban. Mick draped around Todd's thigh and Stephen chose Todd's neck to coil around, encircling it tenderly. The worm was like a warm, living scarf.

Todd settled into his seat, even as he had his pick of them, being careful not to squish his new, wriggly friends. They all shifted their positions to allow him to lean back in the seat as Mick moved to his lap and covered the entirety of it, even when coiled into three loops. Todd estimated Mick, like the others, had grown to at least three feet long and more than four inches thick. He ran his fingertips down Mick's back. Mick liked it as much as Socrates had.

Todd doubted he would have any trouble at the airport. If he did, his new companions would help him. There was a drug dealer with a shit-ton of heroin that Todd needed. He imagined his visit with Dumps would be quite interesting and, if the worms decided Todd was food after all, at least he would be too high to care. And who knew? Maybe his squiggly friends wouldn't mind being high, too.

The plane descended with no announcement. Just as Todd had figured, the crew in the sealed off compartment knew something was wrong. Many vehicles with flashing lights littered the runway and Todd was sure the pilot would head straight for them, stopping the plane just before them, allowing for quick access to it.

The bodies on the floor near Todd swelled more. Some pulsated. They were getting ready to blow. Perhaps what would emerge would be even bigger than the worms with Todd, creatures larger and stronger, more able to handle the emergency personnel who waited, aware of an issue but never able to comprehend the horror they would soon face.

The plane touched down. The body of the first infected man throbbed with vigour. His shirt tore under the force of his expanding chest and belly, and small buttons flew to ping off seats before hitting the floor. His exposed skin stretched, and a fissure broke the surface, from his throat to past his belly button. It looked like a jagged crack opened in the ground by an earthquake only this one was bloody. That smell surfaced again, the mixture of shit and dead things, but it didn't disgust Todd any longer. The worms had a faint hint of that smell, he supposed their natural scent, and he had grown accustomed to it.

Inside the fissure, dark bodies squirmed and writhed, moving over one another like a ball of courting snakes. There couldn't be anything left in the man but them. He had been an awesome incubator. How many squiggled inside him, ready to make their appearance? Dozens, for sure. And in all the passengers on the plane? Hundreds, certainly. An army of hungry worms Todd had no doubt were eager to find new incubators. A legion of new companions for him, ready to do his bidding.

Todd grinned. Socrates lifted a head that also sported a grin.

"Ready to rock, little buddy? Here we go ..."

Grinders

Mark Deloy

Margaret was almost finished with her nightly duties. The morgue was the final area she had left to clean. She always saved the morgue for last.

Her custodial job at Everett Regional included cleaning the first floor and basement offices, which mostly consisted of taking out the trash, vacuuming, and cleaning the bathrooms. All that was fine, much better than working up in the ICU, or even worse, the Colonoscopy Unit. Margaret shivered involuntarily, then smiled. She'd been cleaning for a living for most of her adult life. At sixteen, she was working at the chain motels that mostly employed illegals and paid next to nothing. Then she got a cushy job cleaning corporate offices in Brentwood overnight. That was a good job, but working third shift played hell with her insomnia. So she'd taken this second shift job six months ago, and it had been mostly a breeze. Except for that damned morgue.

She pushed her cart up to the double doors and scanned her badge to open them. The panel beeped, and the doors swung inward, opening into the dimly lit corridor. No one was working right now. She looked at her watch. 11:50 PM. Technically, she had two hours left on her shift, but the morgue didn't take long to clean. She'd be done in no time and could spend her last hour scrolling through Facebook.

All she had to do was empty the three wastebaskets, one near the door, one in the small office in the back, and one in the cold room. The cold room was used for receiving, preparation and temporary storage of cadavers. Lastly, she had to mop the cold room floor.

Tonight, the morgue contained three cadavers sealed in black body bags and sitting on the stainless-steel tables. She was used to seeing the bagged corpses and ignored them for the most part, but she did tend to work a bit faster when the dead were present.

She never read the tags. The ID tags were visible behind clear plastic windows on the side of each bag. If she read the tags, then the bodies had names, were real people, who'd had real lives. Her greatest fear was that one night she would come in here to clean and see a child-sized bag laying on one of the tables. It hadn't happened yet, but she knew it was inevitable. Kids died just like everyone else.

When she finished vacuuming the office, she looked at her watch and saw she was slightly ahead of schedule. At this rate she would have 45 minutes to sit, put her feet up, and get paid to waste time. The Medical Records office was right across the hall and there was a couch in the director's office where she could hide out for the rest of her shift. She just had to mop the refrigerated storage room while trying not to glance at any of the ID tags.

The cold room consisted of ten long term storage drawers along the wall, and five stainless steel examining tables. Three of which were presently occupied.

Margaret filled her mop bucket using the extension nozzle hanging over the stainless-steel sinks. She tried not to imagine what had washed down those drains. She was supposed to use the water hose in the janitor's closet down the hall, but this was another reason why she had 45 minutes to relax at the end of her shift. She was efficient and knew how to save time.

When she finished filling the wheeled mop bucket, she attached the mop ringer to the side, dunked the mop into the soapy water and used the mop handle to push it to the far side of the room. The bucket's wheels bumped and squeaked over the tiles, the sound echoed in the sterile room giving her the willies.

She finished half the room and started mopping under the first steel table, slopping the strong disinfectant soapy water onto the green ceramic tiles.

Margaret caught movement out of the corner of her eye. At first, she thought it was her imagination. She stopped mopping and stared at the black human-shaped lump closest to her. Nothing. She was about to start mopping again when something beneath the bag moved again. Something was alive in there.

Margaret whimpered softly. She'd heard that bodies could move after death, gasses were emitted during decomposition, nerves still fired as if resisting the stillness of death. But this wasn't a fart or a quick twitch of an arm or a leg, this was steady movement as if there was something else in there with the body.

That was when she heard the sound. The grind.

When her son, Chad still lived at home, Margaret woke up to the strangest sound one night. The first time she heard it, she laid in bed for ten minutes wondering what it was until she could take it no longer and had to investigate. She traced the sound to her son's room and realized he was grinding his teeth. When they talked to Chad's doctor about it, he got Chad a mouthguard and he'd eventually stopped. The sound she was hearing now, coming from beneath thick black plastic, was that same sound. Teeth grinding.

Whatever was in there continued to move. Margaret knew she should turn around and run out of here and find a new job, perhaps cleaning restaurants downtown. But she was hypnotized. She had to know what was moving around in there. She steeled herself and sucked in a lungful of Lysol scented air. She had no idea how long this person (body), she told herself, had been dead. Then she gripped the heavy tab before she could think too much about it and pulled. The loud ziiiiip echoed in the still space. She flung the bag open to let the smell dissipate, like she'd seen medical examiners do on TV. What they never show on TV is sometimes there are things inside that have turned to liquid, and sometimes those liquids get on the inside of the bag. So, when said bag is flung open....

Cold jellied goo slopped onto Margaret's cheek and neck. Some of it landed in her hair. The smell instantly hit her, and she gagged, frantically wiping her skin and smearing whatever was in her hair along her forehead. She gagged again and finally got herself under control. Her eyes were watering, and she was desperately trying not to take any breaths through her nose. She closed her eyes, steeled herself and looked back at the body.

What she saw made no sense. Surely this wasn't what happened to all decomposing bodies. Maggots weren't that big. She'd never seen even lawn grubs that big, although these things looked exactly like huge grubs. But these were so fucking big, and there were so many of them, and they were eating.....

The corpse's legs were completely gone up to his hairy thighs. Margaret could see the man's white femurs poking out of the mangled stumps. The worms writhed over the meat and covered the slime-covered stainless-steel table. The creatures were thick and segmented like the Michelin Man, their yellowish-white skin stretched tight from the meal they'd just eaten.

The maggots' mandibles worked furiously against the bones. They had burrowed deep into the marrow. One of them poked its nightmare head out of the jagged pipe of bone as if to say, "Hi there, bitch, you're next."

Several of the globulous worms had retreated from the man's ruined legs and were now at the bottom of the table spurting out egg after egg like some grotesque assembly line. The eggs were the color of caterpillar guts swirled with phlegm.

The eggs sat motionless for a few seconds, then they quivered and burst open, spilling a baby nightmare onto the table. The creatures instantly smelled the rotting meat and heard their brothers' ravenous mastication. They slithered up to the corpse's ruined legs to get their first taste of human flesh.

The sound of them devouring the man's corpse was everywhere now. It was like thunder or a motorcycle engine in the distance.

A deep searing pain exploded in Margaret's shoulder and she looked down, instantly knowing what she would see. A bloom of red on her white uniform spread like a flower around a ragged hole.

She screamed, and frantically batted at the hole, now feeling the worm inside of her shoulder. It slithered and chewed, working its way deep into her. She felt faint but willed herself to stay conscious. If she passed out, she was dead, no doubt about it. She had to get that thing out of her, NOW!

There was a package of disposable medical instruments sitting on a wheeled tray next to the body. Margaret grabbed them, knowing she would likely only have one shot.

She bit a corner of the package and felt the hard edge of one of the tools bangs against her front teeth. The bag stretched, then tore open.

Suddenly Margaret felt intense pressure in the wound and had to catch her breath as another wave of nausea and light-headedness washed over her. She took another quick hitching breath and focused on getting the fucking package open.

Her fingers poked into the bag, searching, trying to snag one of the tools in a pincer between her index and ring fingers. She should have torn a larger hole, but there was no time to think about that now. She finally snagged a pair of forceps and managed to pull them out.

Next was her shirt. She was glad she hadn't worn scrubs tonight. They were allowed to, but tonight she'd opted for a button-down. She tore at it and felt the button pop free and shoot across the room.

Margaret steeled herself, took a deep breath and jammed the forceps into the wound. As she did, she felt the worm wriggle inside of her, trying to escape the instrument. A sharper pain exploded in Margaret's shoulder. Her arm sagged sending bolts of exquisite agony up her neck and down her arm. She realized what must've just happened. The huge maggot had chewed right through her collarbone.

Margaret screamed again and jammed the forceps deeper into the bloody hole. The ragged flesh and raw nerves burned as if she'd used a blowtorch on herself. She opened the tool inside of her and felt the soft skin of the maggot burst open. She gripped the creature and pulled slowly, hoping to get the whole thing. She suddenly had a horrific vision of the maggot tearing in half and half of it still inside of her, chewing, grinding through bone and eventually burrowing into her heart.

At first, Margaret didn't think she'd be able to get it out. It didn't budge. But as she slowly pulled, she felt the creature let go. The gore covered slimy grub slid out of her and there was instant relief. She held it up. It was still wriggling between the forceps' grip. Then she flung it across the room where it splattered against one wall.

As she turned to go, Margaret felt another bolt of intense pain in her right leg, just below her knee. She looked down and saw a ragged bloody hole in her right shin. Another maggot must've fallen off the table and crawled up her leg as she struggled with the one in her shoulder.

There was another loud crack as Her right tibia snapped in half. The maggot had quickly crewed through the bone with its powerful jaws. Margaret collapsed to the floor, scrambling across the floor as more of the creatures slithered up her legs. They began to feed on the soft muscled flesh of her calves and thighs.

She desperately tried to make it to the doors, smearing her blood across the tile floor. Margaret began to whimper softly. One of the creatures had made it to the edge of her white cotton panties and she could feel it starting to chew at the elastic there. She had seconds before the situation went from horrible to unimaginable.

She rolled over and squished the maggot that was trying get inside her. Its cold wet guts slid down Margaret's thigh as she clawed at the wall. She finally managed to lift herself high enough to use her security badge.

The door beeped and swung open onto the main hallway, but now Margaret was getting dizzy again. She had lost a lot of blood. Her vision started to darken and fuzz at the edges. She felt her bowels let go. The maggots began to feed on her shit along with the rest of her. Her last thought just before the maggots chewed through the base her skull, was of the mess she was leaving and who would have to clean it up.

***

Christine Durham scanned her badge and opened the door to the basement offices. The Medical Records office where she worked was at the end of the corridor. She hoped she was the first one in this morning and could enjoy her first cup of French Roast in peace.

As she walked past the morgue, she noticed one of the double doors was standing open. She hurried past, hoping she wouldn't encounter any orderlies wheeling dead bodies off the elevator.

She liked coming in early because she got a lot done but having to walk past the morgue with no one else around and in the dark was not one of her favorite things.

She looked at her watch. It was ten after six. She had an hour to sip her coffee and read email before her office manager, Tiffany got there and started asking a never-ending flood of questions.

Christine plugged her laptop into the docking station, booted it up took a sip of her coffee. She opened Outlook and scanned through random messages from department heads and doctors, looking for any task she couldn't put off until later.

She printed a medical record she needed to file and got up to retrieve it off the printer. As she came out of her office and walked past the office door, she saw something moving on the carpet under the door. It looked like a Styrofoam packing peanut, but then it moved again and slithered further into the office. It was followed by another, then a third.

Christine bent down to get a closer look. She wasn't usually afraid of creepy crawlers, but these things were gross. She was going to have to call an exterminator.

She grabbed the broom and dustpan from the small storage closet near the front desk, then opened the door so she could scoop up any left in the hall as well. Hopefully, she could get all of them.

When Christine pushed the door open, she first thought someone had dumped a bucket of soapy water into the hallway. The floor roiled and moved like flotsam and jetsam, the mass spreading down the hall like a wave. The left branch of the hallway led to admitting, the right, dead-ended on the Emergency room the burn unit, and critical care.

Christine realized the floor was alive with those things. They were moving along the walls as well as the floor.

As the realization of what she was seeing dawned on her, Christine began to hear the first screams and shocked gasps from the ER.

There was another sound as well. The monotonous grinding, like the rumble of an approaching storm.

Mr. Melty-Face

John Barackman

Four Star General, and member of the Joint Chiefs of Staff, Arthur F. Baethan was sitting at his desk on the fifth floor of the Pentagon building in Arlington, Virginia. Behind him was a panoramic view out the General's window of the green grass and white headstones of the Arlington National Cemetery. Across the General's desk sat Lieutenant Douglas H. Nathrach, Assistant Director of the Intelligence Division, Federal Bureau of Investigation. On the desktop was resting an old-fashioned reel-to-reel audio tape recorder.

"Please be as concise as possible Lieutenant, I have a meeting with the President in two hours and I want to be able to give him a cogent report when asked," said General Baethan in a clipped tone.

"As you wish, General."

"I understand Lieutenant, you recently traveled to San Francisco and have material evidence to show me that will help explain the current situation we have ongoing on the west coast. In particular our loss of communication with all command and control units including non-military and governmental. You may or may not be aware of this, but due to the serious threat this poses, the President is holed up in his emergency underground bunker awaiting my assessment of the situation."

"Yes General. I have with me a set of materials: voice recordings, surveillance camera footage, satellite data, transcripts of interviews, etc., which should provide the kind of clarity you are looking for. I would like to start at the beginning; the first contact with our Person of Interest No.1 and the subsequent events leading from that first contact to the present time."

"Very good. You may begin when ready Lieutenant."

"What you are about to hear General, is an interview conducted on..." Lieutenant Nathrach dug out a small notepad from his front shirt pocket, "...let's see now – on April fourteenth of this year. Approximately three months back."

"Jesus. Only three months from barely a blip to this mess," interrupted General Baethan with a solemn shake of his head.

Lieutenant Nathrach cleared his throat then continued:

"These are statements made, it is believed, by the first person to survive long enough to document his experiences with Person of Interest No. 1, also known as 'Mr. Melty-Face.'

"The interviewee is one Simon Pilchard, a professional tailor and owner of Pilchard & Pilchard Clothiers, a maker of high-end suits for men, located in the Financial District of San Francisco, California. It is believed it was because Mr. Pilchard lived in the Miracoma District of San Francisco, and his general thrifty nature, that he was in the habit of taking the Bay Area Rapid Transit system between his home and place of business...

"But, that aside... Mr. Pilchard and the interviewer are the two voices you will hear on this recording.

The Lieutenant carefully rotated the reel-to-reel clockwise on the desk top surface, directing the speakers towards the General. He then depressed the play button. The tape began to spool, and the tinny sounds of recorded voices could be heard:

"I was standing on the BART ramp at the Embarcadero station; I was on my way home." said the recorded voice of Mr. Pilchard.

The voice of the interviewer interrupted Mr. Pilchard: "For the record, this was the Bay Area Rapid Transit system; and you were waiting for a train to transport you to South San Francisco where you live. Is that correct Mr. Pilchard? And this was after work? So, this was what – five p.m. or thereabouts?"

"Yes. Correct. The station was underground, and the lighting was rather dim, but as I looked over from where I was waiting for the train, I saw him standing by himself near the tracks."

"Him?" the interviewer questioned.

"Yes. Him. As I said, he was near the tracks not twenty feet from where I stood so I got a good look at him... and he was... um... difficult to look at."

"How do you mean, 'difficult to look at,' Mr. Pilchard?"

"I mean his face and hands looked... well... melted. Horribly burned. Like someone had used a welding torch on him.

"He had only small scattered tufts of hair on his head, and his nose was completely gone. Burnt off. The nose holes in his skull were the only things remaining.

"A small nub of ear lobe remained on the left side of his head, and his right ear lobe was missing altogether.

"One eye was burned away; just an empty eye socket remained. The other eye looked to have been cooked while his eye was partially open; you could still see the eyeball, but it was shriveled and white. I naturally assumed he was totally blind.

"His mouth had been burned to a snarl of teeth, and his skin appeared paper thin and bubbly, like his head was covered in lumpy white putty just barely covering his skull.

"His right hand was totally missing – an arm bone stuck out where his wrist used to be. The index finger of his left hand, withered and deformed, was all that remained of it. The finger twitched reflexively..."

There was a pause in the taped dialog for a moment.

"Go on Mr. Pilchard. I know this must be difficult, but I appreciate any information you can provide," said the interviewer, his voice calming.

"Well... Like I said, I had noticed him standing by the track. It was then that he turned and looked right at me."

"Looked right at you Mr. Pilchard? I thought you said he was totally blind."

"I distinctly felt him 'looking' at me. I swear I could feel it!" The voice of Mr. Pilchard rose with emotion.

"It's okay Mr. Pilchard. I believe you. Please continue."

"While I was distracted by him 'looking' at me, I failed to notice the other guy approach."

"Another burn victim approached you?" asked the interviewer.

"I was approached by someone, but not a burn victim. He was normal, except he wasn't... I mean he was strange."

"Strange Mr. Pilchard? In what way?"

"He spoke to me. But when he spoke it was like he was reading from a script. And what he said was... not normal."

"What did he say to you?"

"He said: 'Hello Mr. Pilchard. Allow me to introduce myself: I'm the representative of Mr. Melty-Face. He has asked me to convey a message to you – he would like you to make him a suit.' The strange man pointed to the burned guy as he said 'Mr. Melty-Face' so I knew that was whom he was referring to.

"I thought to myself, 'What an odd thing to say...'" continued Mr. Pilchard.

"I was wearing one of my finest suits that day, which I usually did when I was in the store for the day – this being my approach to marketing my product.

"But, I thought, his name is 'Mr. Melty-Face?' What kind of name is that? And how in the hell does he know I'm a tailor? And how did he know my name? I wouldn't forget meeting someone like that! He wants me to tailor a suit for him?"

"So, what did you tell this 'representative of Mr. Melty-Face'?" The voice of the interviewer indicated he was beginning to think Mr. Pilchard was mentally unstable.

"It was at that moment that I noticed Mr. Melty-Face was standing just to the right of me, not a foot in distance away."

"How did he find his way over to you Mr. Pilchard? He's blind, correct? Did he follow your voice? Explain to me how that was possible..." The interviewer was sounding more incredulous by the moment.

"I don't know. But there he was next to me. He touched me in the chest, and after a brief moment of pain, I understood things much clearer. I went back to the factory and made Mr. Melty-Face a very fine suit if I don't say so myself. I made suits for all his associates as well."

Lieutenant Nathrach reached over and punched the off button to the reel-to-reel.

"This is where it gets weird General, and I have to warn you, uncomfortable to listen to."

"Uncomfortable? How do you mean uncomfortable?" queried General Baethan.

"You'll see. But it will probably help explain at least some of the observations about our situation on the West Coast," answered Lieutenant Nathrach.

The Lieutenant hit the play button again.

The interviewer's voice from the recording continued: "After a brief moment of pain? Then you understood what Mr. Pilchard? What do you mean you made him a suit? What associates are you referring to Mr. Pilchard? You are not making any sense here – please explain things to me, one thing at a time if you would." It was clear that the interview was not going as expected and the interviewer was becoming flummoxed.

To this Mr. Pilchard replied, "It would be easier, I believe, if my manager, Mr. Melty-Face, explained things to you personally. Please look out your window..."

General Baethan could hear the squeak of a chair followed by footsteps, then the exclamation in the interviewer's voice: "Oh my God! It's him! How did he get into the locked parking area of our building? This is a secured facility! Wait. What the… Where did he go? He just vanished – one minute he was there then the next poof!"

"Sorry to interrupt, but if you would please turn around and face the interior of the room once more... Mr. Melty-Face is standing right behind you – he will answer all of your questions."

There was a brief pause in the voice recording then a sharp gasp.

The voice of Mr. Pilchard continued: "There you go. Thank you. But before we begin, Mr. Melty-Face would like me to tell you something important. What he wants me to tell you is this: 'Don't worry; it will only hurt for a moment...'"

There was another brief moment of silence heard from the tape recording, then:

"No! Please don't touch me! No! No! Oh God! OW! OWWWWAAAAARRRRR!!!!..."

The awful, agonizing scream turned into an electronic hum after about thirty seconds, and then the recording went silent.

Lieutenant Nathrach hit the off button for the last time. "That's about all there is I'm afraid General," he said.

General Baethan reached into his desk, pulled out a bottle of antacids, twisted off the cap, pulled two tablets out of the bottle, and popped them into his mouth, swallowing hard. He declared with no small amount of consternation, "Wait just a cotton-pickin' minute there Lieutenant Nathrach! What in God's name was that high-pitched hum, and how the hell did this 'Mr. Melty-Face' get into that office? Entry to that building is guarded, for the Love of Christ, by armed guards twenty-four seven!"

"That was the sound of the microphone melting; it was placed too near the interviewer – thank God the recorder was at a sufficient distance from the heat when it all went down, or we would not have had that recording. And as for the rest, well, I have a video sequence to show you from a surveillance camera that may help explain things," replied Lieutenant Nathrach.

"Very well Lieutenant, you may proceed," said General Baethan only slightly calmed.

Lieutenant Nathrach moved the reel-to-reel out of the way, pulled a laptop computer from his briefcase, and placed the laptop on the desktop where the reel-to-reel had sat. He opened the cover, clicked on the keyboard a moment, and then rotated the laptop so the screen could be viewed by the General.

"What I am about to show you, General, is the video feed from a surveillance camera used by the BART police to monitor the Embarcadero station platform. The camera was mounted at ceiling level in the Southwest corner and tilted downward to afford a view of the entire platform. The camera was at the perfect angle and distance to record the activities surrounding Mr. Pilchard. Lucky for us it was a full color high-res camera, so the playback was of sufficient resolution to show us clearly the activities as they happened. The clip of footage I will show you began a few minutes before Mr. Simon Pilchard was approached by Person of Interest No.1 and his so-called 'Representative'."

Lieutenant Nathrach walked around to the side of General Baethan's desk to get better access to the laptop's keyboard. He clicked the key that would make the video play forward. General Baethan leaned in to get a closer view of the screen.

"Over here General, you can see where Mr. Pilchard is standing," tapping on the laptop screen to illustrate Mr. Pilchard's placement in the video image, "and to his right about twenty five feet away you can see the individual who called himself the 'Representative' sitting down at a bench," tap, tap, tap, on the screen, "And finally, Person of Interest No.1 himself right over there," pointing to a man at the very lower corner of the screen. His face and body were turned perpendicular to Mr. Pilchard but in direct line of sight of the camera.

"I can see what that Simon Pilchard fellow was meaning by 'he's difficult to look at' – Person of Interest No.1 has a face only a mother could love," said General Baethan with a chuckle.

"Pay attention closely General, this is going to get interesting very fast..."

General Baethan leaned forward once again to look at the video playback.

"Okay, here you can see Mr. Pilchard has noticed Person of Interest No. 1. You see Mr. Pilchard staring at him long and hard," continued Lieutenant Nathrach, "assuming, as one would naturally assume, I suppose, that Person of Interest No. 1 cannot see him staring."

"Here it is... Right here... The so called 'Mr. Melty-Face' rotates slowly until he is facing Mr. Pilchard. At this same moment, the so called 'Representative' stands up and walks over to Mr. Pilchard. Here you can see that, at the precise instant that the Representative reached Mr. Pilchard, the Representative began to say something to him that catches his attention. There! His lips are now moving and Mr. Pilchard, distracted from his examination of Mr. Melty-Face, turns to look in the direction of the Representative's voice. This is when... there! Mr. Melty-Face appears directly to the right of Mr. Pilchard."

"Whoa! Hold y'r horses there a minute part'ner! We're missing some frames in the playback! I just saw our Person of Interest No. 1 travel twenty-five feet in a second... not possible!" exclaimed General Baethan.

"Let me back this video up to the moment prior to this General... Okay. I paused it to the second before Person of Interest No. 1's movement across the BART platform. I will step through the sequence frame by frame. Look at the time signatures at the bottom. The camera was recording at thirty frames per second, so that translates to approximately thirty-four milliseconds per frame," explained Lieutenant Nathrach.

Clicking the keyboard to step through the video frame-by-frame, the General watched as Person of Interest No. 1 slowly rotated about to face Mr. Pilchard.

Lieutenant Nathrach continued: "You will note that no frames are missing – the time signatures are contiguous. And here we are to the critical few frames – in the first frame I'm showing you here General, Person of Interest No. 1 is where he was down by the tracks, and in the very next frame, he is a foot from Mr. Pilchard."

"Mr. Melty-Face moved twenty five feet in thirty four milliseconds?" asked General Baethan, his face screwed up in a 'What the Hell!' expression, "that would be..." quickly running through the calculation in his head, "just under five hundred miles per hour Lieutenant. That's not possible."

"No General, the camera was simply too slow to capture his true speed. Our work has shown us that Person of Interest No. 1 moves across distances, sometimes vast distances, instantaneously."

"So, what do we have here? Proof of time travel? Wormholes? Instantaneous matter transfer through space? Is that what your Intelligence Division at the FBI is claiming, Lieutenant Nathrach, or are you a lone wolf out on a limb here?"

"The Intelligence Community, General, has studied this phenomenon thoroughly and we are in perfect agreement on this. Not only is Person of Interest No. 1 able to instantaneously jump twenty-five feet, we have reason to believe, and the video footage to back it up, that he has leapt instantaneously to both San Diego, California, and to Seattle, Washington.

"In fact, we are in agreement that Person of Interest No. 1 is not from here."

"Not from here? You are saying this is some kind of alien invasion?" The General said with stern alarm as he reached into his desk and popped a few more antacids into his mouth.

"Not alien. But not from Earth either... From somewhere else."

"Somewhere else? What the hell does that mean?" exclaimed an incredulous General Baethan as he chewed his antacid tablets.

"That is the FBI's official designation of source of origin for our Person of Interest No. 1: 'Somewhere Else.' Probably from somewhere hot. Very hot," replied Lieutenant Nathrach evenly.

"Somewhere hot! Oh, for the love of God! Can you please say something that makes even a little sense? The so called 'Intelligence Community' should be able to make sense of things!" yelled the General.

General Baethan felt the urge to throw something at the Lieutenant, but he steadied his nerves and said instead, "Oh for the Love of Christ... Please go on Lieutenant..."

The General pulled out a handkerchief from his pocket and wiped his face. Sweat had begun to break out on the General's forehead.

"The next few minutes of video playback will help to explain General," said Lieutenant Nathrach as he hit the key to continue the playback.

"As I previously pointed out, if you watch carefully, you will see that the Representative leans in towards Mr. Pilchard and speaks to him. Wait for it... There!" Lieutenant Nathrach quickly clicked the key to halt the playback, "It is important to note what this 'Representative' told Mr. Pilchard at that moment. We asked several professional lip readers to analyze this sequence and they all confirmed the following to be the case. What he said was: 'Don't worry, it will only hurt for a moment.'

"Don't worry, it will only hurt for a moment?" repeated General Baethan, "Wasn't that what Mr. Pilchard said to the interviewer?"

"Yes. The phase: 'Don't worry, it will only hurt for a moment,' is said by all Representatives just before a transformation is to be inflicted on a victim.

"Clarify for me Lieutenant, just how did Mr. Pilchard become a representative for our Person of Interest No. 1? And transformation? What in God's Green Earth does that mean? Something people do in a hippy-dippy new-age sleep over?" The General's voice rose in anger as he talked. He pulled out the handkerchief once again and wiped his face, "Jesus H. Christ on a Cross! What the hell am I going to tell the President?" he mumbled as he wiped.

"Yes. Transformation. It means 'the act of change,' and it is the term the Intelligence Community came up to describe what follows one being touched by a Melty-Face.

"The rest of the video play will illustrate this..."

Lieutenant Nathrach once again clicked the key to run the video playback. General Baethan watched the screen as Person of Interest No. 1 raised his left hand and touched Mr. Pilchard in the middle of his chest with his one remaining finger. Mr. Pilchard instantly burst forth in bright flames that surrounded his entire body. Mr. Pilchard began to dance frantically, his arms flailing about wildly. There was no soundtrack to accompany the video feed, but if there had been, General Baethan was sure he would have heard mad screaming. Through the curtain of flame, Mr. Pilchard's face was a mask of pure agony, his mouth wide open in a howling scream, his tongue darting in and out. Large billows of black smoke rolled off Mr. Pilchard as he thrashed about. A minute rolled by. Then suddenly, the flames simply died as if they were snuffed out with water. Mr. Pilchard stopped dancing and stood calmly with his arms at his side. General Baethan was surprised that he appeared to be untouched by the flames: no burnt flesh, no visible damage at all. His suit was intact. Mr. Pilchard then looked up and stared directly into the surveillance camera. He smiled a tight smile at the lens. Then suddenly he turned away and walked out of the frame of the camera, the Representative and Person of Interest No. 1 following close behind.

"That is the end of this sequence, General.

"Our research has shown that when one is touched by Person of Interest No. 1, or one of his clones for that matter, you are either transformed into a Representative, another 'Mr. Melty-Face' clone, or a pile of ash. Most victims of transformation are converted to ash," explained Lieutenant Nathrach.

"Clones! There are more of these, um… things?!" said General Baethan, fear more than anger now written over his face.

Lieutenant Nathrach did not immediately answer; instead he sat in his seat and rotated the laptop around so that the screen again faced him. He tapped on the keyboard a minute, and then rotated it back around to face General Baethan. He got up and stepped back to his spot at the side of the desk.

"Here is the same BART surveillance camera two days after that first interaction with Mr. Pilchard," said Lieutenant Nathrach as he punched the key to play the video.

Standing on the train platform were a dozen Mr. Melty-Faces, and an equal number of Representatives. They did not appear to be moving, only standing silently in place, as if waiting for a cue to begin.

"Notice the beautiful blue suits the Melty-Faces are wearing! All made by Mr. Pilchard, naturally. Such quality..." exclaimed Lieutenant Nathrach, as if he found joy in such a thing.

General Baethan put away the comment about the suits temporarily, instead he asked, "There are now twelve? They're spreading?"

"Not long after this video was taken, surveillance cameras in several other locations, notably in the San Diego, San Francisco, and Seattle areas showed multiple Melty-Faces spontaneously appearing. These are all assumed to be clones of Person of Interest No. 1.

"Hummm… The precise areas that we have lost contact with..." surmised General Baethan, "But all of those areas have populations in the millions. How did they get overwhelmed so quickly? By a dozen Melty-Faces?"

"Exponential growth General. We asked Doctor Janise L. Albrecht, a Professor of Mathematics at MIT, to estimate the rate of growth and number of days to transform the roughly fifteen million residents of the combined greater San Diego, San Francisco, and Seattle metropolitan areas. Her answer was a few months would be all it would take. She used the following satellite imagery to help her make that estimate..."

Lieutenant Nathrach once again sat in his seat, rotated the laptop around to face him, tapped on the keyboard, and rotated it back around to face General Baethan.

"The image you see is of the California interstate I-5 freeway, the portion of which carries the bulk of commuters between the Los Angeles basin and that of the greater San Diego area. It represents approximately eighty miles of freeway. At the time this satellite image was recorded, it was smack dab in the middle of evening rush hour on a Thursday commute day. This would place the event four days post first contact with Person of Interest No. 1. The image has been enhanced to highlight both cars and people in blue. You can see that the freeway is packed with cars. Most are moving at only a few miles-per-hour due to the heavy congestion. We estimate that there were over two hundred thousand cars on the freeway at that moment, and, at an approximate 1.2

people per car, over two hundred fifty thousand commuters in those same said cars.

"Here we go... At the southernmost portion of the freeway, near downtown San Diego, it begins... You see those red dots appear? Those are satellite enhanced Melty-Face clones. Probably thirty clones to start with. Watch as they transform the first set of victims. You see that! White flashes? Those are the heat trails from the immolation of their victims. One minute later... Bang! You can now see that the size of the area occupied by the red dots has doubled.

"We have determined that there are an equal number of Representatives being created as well, but they are not shown on this video sequence for clarity purposes."

As General Baethan was watching the action on the screen, his stomach knotted with anxiety. The antacids were not doing their job.

Lieutenant Nathrach hit the pause key temporarily.

He continued: "For purposes of scale, a centimeter of the computer screen at this level of magnification is equivalent to roughly three point eight miles of distance along the freeway. It starts slowly but grows exponentially. It is like a fuse is lit General." He hit the play key again.

The video showed the red dots and white flares grew slowly at first as the event progressed from the southernmost end of the interstate, but then quickly picked up speed as the number of red dots grew and the white flares of immolation spread up the freeway, becoming an explosion of activity as the minutes ticked by.

"We estimate, even with only a few percent of those transformed into Melty-Faces, the vast majority of those victims being turned to ash – that within thirty minutes, the entire length of the interstate was transformed."

"I see blue dots, red dots, and white flairs blossoming out both sides of the freeway, like things are spilling out into the surrounding neighborhoods. What is happening there?" asked General Baethan.

"Those are people fleeing their cars General, to get away from the wave of Melty-Faces coming their way. I suppose the burning to death of so many people right in front of one would inspire one to run for one's life don't you agree General? But it didn't help those poor slobs. The Melty-Faces quickly caught up to them despite their fleeing. It was like they were 'marked' for transformation. Their time was simply up.

"It might not be obvious, General, so I will point this out, but clogging this, as well as the multitude of other metropolitan freeway systems in an analogous manner, with the burnt carcasses of cars in the aftermath of mass transformation, had the double whammy of preventing escape for those yet to be transformed still hiding out in their homes and offices. Very sad…"

"So, I suppose the multitude of Melty-Faces being created here is each given a 'beautiful blue suit' to wear?" This was an attempt at humor by General Baethan, albeit morbid humor, but to his surprise, Lieutenant Nathrach answered:

"Well, no General, our research has shown that the suits can't be made fast enough, unfortunately. Our spies have found that the Representative formally known as Mr. Pilchard is ramping up production of the blue suits as fast as possible, but he has been running into issues with labor shortages. I failed to mention the women… Although all children under sixteen years, and nearly all women for that matter, were reduced to ash during their transformation process, a rather large number, we estimate in the thousands, of the women that encountered a Melty-Face were not transformed at all, but were instead rounded up and made to work as seamstresses within Mr. Pilchard's factory. Production has been ramping up to match the demand rather quickly. Each Melty-Face has been, and will continue to be, provided a suit in no time at all."

"Women forced to perform work as seamstresses? What is this, the industrial revolution?" asked General Baethan, his voice cracking from the stress.

"We think Mr. Melty-Face is simply being efficient with the resources he has at hand General."

"I don't know if I can take much more of this Lieutenant," said General Baethan, his head dropping into his hands. He raised his head again after a moment and added, "Unfortunately? You think it's unfortunate that these blue suits can't be manufactured with sufficient speed to clothe all of these murderous invaders?"

"A poor choice of words General. Horrific as this all may be, you've got to admire the speed at which this is all going down. That Mr. Melty-Face is one industrious SOB!"

General Baethan could only give Lieutenant Nathrach an incredulous look.

"So, this rapid spread has led to the collapse of our west coast COMSAT system Lieutenant? And just how did those so called 'Melty-Faces' gain access to those highly secured facilities?"

"It is a fact that facilities that house those of high rank within the military control and command structure, and those within high civilian governmental positions for that matter General, have been targeted early in the transformation process. That seems to be the pattern when a new area is targeted.

"Let me pull up the current view, General, and zoom the satellite imagery out, so you can see the extent of this thing as of today..." said Lieutenant Nathrach as he quickly tapped on the keyboard.

"There you go General; this is the view of the entire Western Seaboard from the southern border with Mexico, up to the northern border with Canada. As you can see, based on the area's shown in red, that much of greater Seattle, San Francisco, and San Diego are gone. Smaller extents of red in the Los Angeles basin, as well as other miscellaneous small areas that are doted here and there – most notably Portland, Oregon, and Las Vegas areas, have been transformed too."

"Jesus. I knew things were bad, but this can only be described as apocalyptic," said General Baethan in a somber tone.

"Yes General. Armageddon is the official term used by the Intelligence Community."

General Baethan swiveled his chair around to look out his office window. At times when he was under stress, he liked to look out into the peaceful green of the Arlington National Cemetery which was located just across the busy South Washington Boulevard from where he sat. The beauty of the perfectly symmetrical headstones dotting the grassy landscape, framed by the large and picturesque deciduous trees, always helped to calm his nerves. From this distance, he could just make out the people walking the graveyard as they visited loved ones lost to wars fought long ago.

"Thank you for your report, Lieutenant Nathrach. I believe I have what I need for my meeting with the President this afternoon. I think what is in order here is to fight fire with fire. I hate to have to do this, but due to the severity and immediacy of this situation and the grave threat to our Nation this represents... I believe we have no other choice but to use nukes. Our nuclear arsenal was never meant to be used on our own population, but..."

As he had continued to absently scan the people walking amongst the gravestones, General Baethan's words caught in his throat; he suddenly spotted him… Standing next to a gravestone and looking directly in his direction… was a Melty-Face. A cold knife of fear raced down the General's spine. There was no doubt in General Baethan's mind that this was Person of Interest No. 1 himself. He swiveled quickly back around to face Lieutenant Nathrach.

"Lieutenant, I don't believe you ever told me the identity of the interviewer at that first meeting with Mr. Pilchard. Who was he Lieutenant?" demanded General Baethan.

"Why General, the interviewer was me. And once my transformation was complete, I understood everything with perfect clarity," answered Lieutenant Nathrach with a queer smile on his face.

With his left hand, General Baethan reached for the loaded gun he had hidden in the upper left-side drawer of his desk. But before his hand could touch the shiny brass handle of the drawer, out the right side of his vision, he saw a man in a blue suit standing next to him. General Baethan immediately knew who it was… It was Him. As General Baethan's head slowly swiveled around to look at Mr. Melty-Face, he felt his bowels loosen. He was truly a horrifying sight to look at. The General let out a sharp gasp.

General Baethan was not entirely surprised when a devilish thought went through his mind as he looked at him; it was as if the thought was not his own but was placed into his mind: What a beautiful suit he wears! Impeccably tailored! The starched white of his dress shirt stands in contrast, but in a very pleasing way, to the navy blue of his blazer and suit pants. The darker blue and white polka dot of his silk tie, tied in a perfect full

Windsor knot, gives the entire ensemble a neat, professional look. Those gold and black onyx cuff links accent his shirt with high style! Black Oxford shoes polished to a high gloss – very impressive!

General Baethan noted that the one remaining finger on Mr. Melty-Face's left hand twitched.

"Before I forget General, there is one last thing Mr. Melty-Face would like me to convey to you before your meeting with the President..." said Lieutenant Nathrach, "He wants me to tell you: 'Don't worry, this will only hurt for a moment.'"

No Salvation

Dusty Davis

I can hear them coming for me from under the floorboards
and inside the walls.
The pitter-patter of feet is getting closer, little sharp teeth
gnashing down the halls.
The horde of vermin are out to devour my soul.
Leaving my body like an empty grave, an unfilled hole.
Beast of four legs with a long tail.
Creatures that will damn me to an eternity in hell.
The filthy rodents that are full of disease.
I would pray, but there is no longer a God left to appease.
There is no salvation for me to find.
For this infestation is only in mind.

Training Day

Charles Lynne

My Coven needs training
They are still young
Compared to my last
I hope this crew is more
sensible than those
That came before them
Numerous things tonight
That have been taught
Will be practiced by them
This isn't just for the kill
It's for the thrill of the hunt
Patience will be needed
Suppression of bloodlust
Will win this day
I chose for them
A very small town
That won't be missed
This will be learned
Such as cleanup after
Night has fallen
Our time has come
Each of my students
Have been instructed
Where to attack and how
If they follow their training
Two hours and done
Window glass breaks
Doors creaking open
Muffled screams fill the air

The sweet smell of
Blood fills the night air
It seems this time
I chose my crew
Of misfits correctly
The sheriff is mine
Since he will be the strongest
However, not that strong
Our training night was done
One last request I had made
Of my Coven before we started
Bring me there more for the family
I was not disappointed.

Printed in Great Britain
by Amazon